THE SEER

LINDA JOY SINGLETON lives in northern California. She has two grown children and a wonderfully supportive husband who loves to travel with her in search of unusual stories.

Linda Joy Singleton is the author of more than twenty-five books, including the series Regeneration, My Sister the Ghost, Cheer Squad, and, also from Llewellyn, Strange Encounters.

Sword Play

LINDA JOY SINGLETON

Llewellyn Publications
Woodbury, Minnesota

Help her...

FIRST EDITION
Second Printing, 2007

Format by Steffani Chambers
Cover design and illustration by Lisa Novak
Editing by Rhiannon Ross

Llewellyn is a registered trademark of Llewellyn Worldwide, Ltd.
The Cataloging-in-Publication Data for *Sword Play* is on file at the Library of Congress.
ISBN 13: 978-0-7387-0880-5
ISBN 10: 0-7387-0880-1
Llewellyn Worldwide does not participate in, endorse, or have any authority or responsibility concerning private business transactions between our authors and the public.

All mail addressed to the author is forwarded but the publisher cannot, unless specifically instructed by the author, give out an address or phone number.

Any Internet references contained in this work are current at publication time, but the publisher cannot guarantee that a specific location will continue to be maintained. Please refer to the publisher's website for links to authors' websites and other sources.

Llewellyn Publications
A Division of Llewellyn Worldwide, Ltd.
2143 Wooddale Drive, Dept. 978-0-7387-0880-5
Woodbury, MN 55125-2989, U.S.A.
www.llewellyn.com

Printed in the United States of America

To Write to the Author

If you wish to contact the author or would like more information about this book, please write to the author in care of Llewellyn Worldwide and we will forward your request. Both the author and publisher appreciate hearing from you and learning of your enjoyment of this book and how it has helped you. Llewellyn Worldwide cannot guarantee that every letter written to the author can be answered, but all will be forwarded. Please write to:

Linda Joy Singleton
% Llewellyn Worldwide
2143 Wooddale Drive, Dept. 978-0-7387-0880-5
Woodbury, Minnesota 55125-2989, U.S.A.

Please enclose a self-addressed stamped envelope for reply, or $1.00 to cover costs. If outside U.S.A., enclose international postal reply coupon.

Many of Llewellyn's authors have websites with additional information and resources.
For more information, please visit our website at
http://www.llewellyn.com

To PF Garrett Loethe
A fellow series book enthusiast, smooth dancer,
and treasured friend.

Also, thanks to my instructor Paul at the
Sacramento Fencing Club, who patiently
answered my questions and taught me
the basics of fencing.

1

Waking up to find a cute guy sitting on your bed might be a dream come true for some girls.

But not me.

Especially when the guy was dead—and some people think I killed him.

Normally ghosts didn't scare me. Coming from a long line of psychics, I'd been weaned on Ghosts, Spirits, and Angels 101. I'd had visions of the future and long chatty conversations with my spirit guide. But this was different. This was Kip.

Seeing him so alive and real—six months after his death—was beyond freaky. Terror sliced through me like a sharp blade.

"Go away!" I shouted, then ducked underneath my pillow, my eyes shut tightly and my heart pounding furiously.

Please let this be a bad dream. Yeah, that must be it. I was having a nightmare or maybe a reaction to the pain medication. I remembered falling asleep, relieved to be out of the hospital and back in my own familiar quilted bed. After surviving a deadly road accident, it was logical that I'd dream about car crashes—including the tragedy that would always haunt me. But that was all in the past. I mean, this could *not* be happening. No way was Kip Hurst in my room.

But when I peeked out, there he was, decked out in his #17 football jersey (which was odd since he'd died in a formal prom tux). Energy flickered around him, making his face seem unnaturally pale while his legs were so transparent that when he stood it looked like he was floating over my bed. A football appeared in his hand and he spun it on his fingertip, grinning at me in that arrogant way I always detested.

"Go away!" I tried again.

With a tilt of his head, he regarded me with wry curiosity.

"Get out of here!"

He tossed the ball so high it disappeared in my dark ceiling.

I stared up, waiting for the football—and my own sanity—to return. Long moments stretched on in eerie silence, then the ball slowly sailed into his hand. Only his energy flickered and his hand wasn't there. The football balanced on its pointy end in empty air. I pinched myself, just to check if I was in fact dreaming. Definitely not a dream.

Kip's hand may have vanished and his legs were see-through, but his grin flashed with a cocky attitude. Clearly he was *not* going away.

Gathering my blankets around me, I scooted upright in bed and faced this ghost from my past. Kip had been a star football player with major league expectations and a gorgeous homecoming king. At my old school, Arcadia High, where sports ruled and had more funding than any other department, Kip was truly royalty.

I wasn't one of Kip's fans. It just seemed to me that jocks were overrated. I mean, what was so great about pummeling players on a field? I hadn't even known Kip, except by reputation . . . until The Vision.

Then why was he here so many months later?

Unless he blamed me . . .

I swallowed hard, then forced out the question I knew I had to ask. "What do you want?"

I barely made out his shadowy hand pointing directly at me.

"Me?" I clawed my blankets. "But it wasn't my fault . . . I tried to warn you."

He moved his mouth, only nothing came out.

"I don't know what you're trying to say, but you don't belong here. You died six months ago. You have to let go and move on."

He gave a firm shake of his head, and that's when I realized he wasn't a ghost. Not in the sense of someone who has died but is stuck on earth due to fear or confusion. He had *already* moved on to the other side. His essence glowed with the warm energy of a spirit. He had come a long way because he'd chosen to visit. But why visit me—the girl who predicted his death, but failed to prevent it?

"What can I do for you?" I spoke softly. "Pass on a message to someone?"

He shook his head.

"Then why are you here?"

He tucked the football under one arm and moved closer in a sweeping glide. No longer did he bulldoze through life, taking up more than his share of space and swaggering with an overblown pride. As a dead guy, he was almost human.

When he opened his mouth, I concentrated on all my senses, especially the sixth one, to listen.

"Sah . . . beeen."

I shivered at the eerie sound of my own name. "I'm listening. What do you want?"

"Help," he whispered.

"You need help?"

"Not . . . me."

"But that's what you just asked."

He shook his head.

"I don't understand." I bit my lip, confused. "I can't help you unless you tell me more. I don't know why you're here . . . what you want from me."

Again, he shook his head. His lips pursed and I sensed frustration.

"Help . . . her."

"Who?"

If he answered, I was unable to hear him. Energy flicked like a short-circuited bulb, then there was a crackling sound. Silence and empty darkness. The only light in my room came from my wall where a clown-face night-light glowed.

Kip was gone, yet the whisper of his last words lingered, echoing in my mind, "Help her, help her. . ."

But I had no idea who "her" was . . .

2

I awoke from a deep sleep to a rumbling purr and soft fur rubbing against my cheek.

"Huh?" I murmured groggily. I peeked out to see white fur and mismatched blue-and-green eyes regarding me impatiently.

Living in the country, I never knew what I'd wake up to. A crowing rooster, mooing cows, bleating goats, or my cat Lilybelle. Sometimes I awoke early simply because great smells like wild flowers and freshly cut hay drifted in through my window. Then there were the not-so-great smells like fresh manure or ripe skunk.

You'd think I'd be used to country smells and sounds after living with my grandmother for half a year. But memories have a way of time traveling so that one moment you're in the here and now, then zap! A thought jumps you back to another time, as if you were in two places at the same time. Like two different people.

If only there were two of me, I thought as I cradled Lilybelle in my arms and hugged her close. *Then one of me could stay here like I want and the other could do what my mother wants.*

In a rush, anxiety struck and I felt as sick inside as I had when Mom had come to visit me in the hospital and told me I had to move back to San Jose.

My first impulse was to argue, "No way! Are you nuts? Leave Nona and all my friends? Forget it."

That's what I wanted to say, but not what happened. Emotions twisted inside me. I was scared of hurting people I cared about yet grateful for this crumb of attention from my mother. So I just nodded.

Mom thought she was doing me a favor, welcoming the "disgraced daughter" back home. There had even been tears in her eyes when she'd hugged me goodbye, which was so not like her. I knew she meant well, but she totally did not get me. She treated me like I was six, rather than sixteen, speaking *at* me rather than *to* me in her queen-addressing-subject tone. I could imagine her wearing a crown and declaring her royal proclamation, "Despite the supreme shame you have brought upon your respectable family, you are now forgiven. You have served out your banishment, and may return to dwell in our home."

Only I didn't want to return.

San Jose wasn't my home anymore. Home was with Nona on her ten-acre farm in Sheridan Valley. My grandmother's farmhouse wasn't spacious like my parents' tri-level stucco home in San Jose, and I'll admit it could use some paint and new carpeting. But this cozy home welcomed me with open doors; the oaks and pines hugging the farmhouse, offering shade when it was too hot and holding off chilling winds in storms. And I didn't want to leave, especially now.

Shadows shifted across my bedroom walls, and instinctively I looked over for reassurance at the cheerful clown night-light. The night-light had been a "get well" gift from my boyfriend Josh when he'd visited me in the hospital. He said to think of him whenever I looked at the big clown smile because he clowned around in a fuzzy wig and floppy shoes when he performed magic tricks for sick kids. It was the perfect gift since I collected night-lights. I displayed this collection (unicorns, angels, cats, angels, dragons, and more) in a glassed case. Each night I plugged in a different night-light, the luminous light warding off night visitors.

Night visitors . . .

These two words shivered through me like a shock wave. Something about last night flickered in my mind . . . a bad dream or memory. Not a solid thought but more of a pit-in-my-gut scared feeling. Goose bumps prickled on my arms and I heard a whisper of a male voice telling me to . . . to what?

I tried hard to give the vague feeling shape, but my thoughts were whiffs of smoke playing tag through my mind. I couldn't bring forth the memory. Whatever happened during the night eluded me. A nightmare, I finally decided. Nothing to worry about—especially when I had more urgent worries.

The biggest, most heart-stabbing worry was my grandmother's failing health. Recently I'd found out Nona had a hereditary disease which stole her memories, and if not treated, she'd lapse into a coma and never wake up. There was a cure, but it had been lost to our family over a hundred years ago. I had been tracking down this remedy (it involved finding four silver charms) with Dominic, the handyman/apprentice who worked for my grandmother. We were close to finding the final charm.

We'd also been getting *close* in another way, which was totally wrong. I hated myself, I hated him, and it had to stop. I mean, I already had a boyfriend. Josh was great—sweet, honest, with a fun sense of humor. Dominic was night-and-day different. More sour than sweet and deep with disturbing secrets I'd only started to uncover. He was so not my type. Yet thinking about him gave me crazy anxiety—heart palpitations, hot flashes, and nausea—like coming down with the flu.

Another thing to worry about . . .

Lilybelle meowed and slapped her tail against my arm. Her way of saying, "I want breakfast. *Now.*"

"Message received," I said with a smile.

But my smile changed to a wince of pain when I pushed the covers off my battered body. I glanced down ruefully at the bandage on my left thigh and the purple-yellow bruises on my arms. Tentatively I ran my fingers over the bandage, bitter reminders of my accident. Dominic had been driving me back from the bus station and swerved his truck to avoid crashing into a wayward cow. He'd missed the cow, but totaled his truck and suffered minor cuts. My injuries were much worse, bringing me way too close to death. I was lucky to be alive.

Lilybelle meowed again, then gracefully sprung off my bed.

"Easy for you to move," I grumbled as I carefully eased my bandaged leg to the floor. "You didn't almost get creamed by a cow."

My cat paused by the door and flicked her tail impatiently, obviously not impressed by my pun or sympathetic to my injuries. Food was her only concern, and now that I thought about it, she had a point. A glance at my silver moon watch and I gasped. I was seriously running late. I'd have to rush breakfast or get a tardy my first day back at school.

Slowly, I hobbled across the room. The meds eased the pain, but left me weak and light-headed. If I wasn't so sick of staying in bed, I might have put off returning to school. But I'd had enough rest in the hospital to last several decades. Besides, staying alone made me think too much, and worry even more. I would rather do ordinary stuff like getting dressed and hanging out with my friends. Anything to avoid dealing with my last conversation with Mom. I kept what she'd said to myself, dreading the awful thing I had to do. But I couldn't put it off any longer.

I had to tell Nona the bad news.

That I was moving out.

On Friday.

3

Telling Nona turned out to be easy. I was surprised to discover she had been worrying about breaking the news to me. I should have realized my mother would have already talked to her. Nona said she was sad to lose me but understood I belonged with my family.

"You are my family," I told her. Tearfully we hugged, and she assured me I was always welcome here.

Unfortunately telling my friends wasn't as easy.

My best friend Penelope Lovell (nicknamed Penny-Love) totally freaked. Usually we walked to school, but she'd borrowed her brother's beat-up station wagon to make my first day back at school easier. Her color theme today was gold; gold eye shadow, gold mesh earrings, gold lycra top with low-rider jeans.

"NO! You can't do this to me!" Penny-Love smacked her palm against the steering wheel, her freckled cheeks flaming as red as her curly hair.

I almost laughed at how everything was always about her. She was such a diva, and somehow that made her even dearer to me. Hanging out together was always a blast. She was like a queen bee at school, privy to the latest buzz sometimes before it even happened. When I'd arrived at school as a new kid, uncertain and uneasy, she'd opened her circle of friends and generously drew me inside. Something clicked and just like that we bonded. As her best friend I could skim the edges of popularity with no personal risk.

But not much longer . . .

Morosely, I stared out the window at country homes and grassy fields where spindly oak branches reached into wide gray-blue skies. No high rises or crowded urban apartments. I'd stretched and spread my wings here, not confined by concrete expectations. I would miss it all so much.

"I forbid you to leave," Penny-Love was saying. "It's completely unacceptable."

"Tell that to my mother."

"Maybe I will."

"No!" I shook my head firmly. "Believe me, it's no use. My dad's a lawyer, yet he can't even win an argument with my mom."

Penny-Love slowed for an intersection where kids hurried across a crosswalk. "But making you leave is just wrong. You'll miss out on everything. What about your grandmother's All Hallows party? It's Friday night."

"I already talked about it with Nona. She wanted to change the date so I could make it, but I wouldn't let her. Why ruin everyone else's fun?"

"Hello? What about *your* fun?" She cupped her ear like she didn't believe what she was hearing. "It's your party, too. You have to be there."

"I can't help it. The party goes on as planned and I'll expect you to tell me all about it afterwards. I feel better knowing you're there to help Nona."

"Helping her is now my official job. After school, I'll start working as her assistant for Soul-Mate Matches. How's this sound for my official job title: Assistant Love Doctor?"

"Penny-Love, Assistant Love Doctor." I smiled. "Perfect."

"I'm thinking of having a badge made. Won't that look cool?"

"Definitely. You're a natural for the romance biz."

"Thanks, Sabine. See that's another reason why you can't leave. No one gets me like you do, and you have a real talent for listening. I don't have time to break in a new best friend. There has to be some way to make you stay."

She kept at me like this until we reached school. It was a relief when she spotted some other friends who waved her over and I was left alone. But I wasn't alone long. At my locker, I found Josh. We had this routine of meeting by my locker before school; something else I'd miss when I moved away.

He looked so happy to see me that I felt a stab of guilt. Before he could say anything, I sucked in a deep breath, then I blurted out everything; how my mom was making me leave even though I'd rather stay here, and how miserable I was. When I'd finished explaining, I braced myself for his reaction.

But Josh just frowned.

"Well say something," I told him. "Are you mad at me?"

"No way. It's not your fault."

"I could have argued and told my mother forget it."

"You're too sweet to disrespect your mother."

Too scared, I thought.

"You did the right thing, Sabine. I really admire that. Most kids think only of themselves and blow off their parents. But you listen and do what they want."

"It's not what I want."

"Me, either." He took my hand, his gentle touch making me feel warm inside. "But I can't blame your parents for wanting you back."

He looked so hot, and standing in the hall by my locker reminded me of the day we met. I'd been lusting after him secretly for weeks without the courage to even say "hi." But after a psychic warning of danger, I was able to save him from a freak auto-shop accident. Gratitude blossomed into something more, and a week later we were officially a couple. Lucky me! Being Josh's girl was sweet and safe. He didn't believe in anything unusual, which was a good balance for my own weirdness.

"It'll be okay, Sabine." Josh leaned close and brushed a kiss on my forehead. "Leaving isn't a tragedy."

"But I'll be over a hundred miles away."

"That's not very far at all, just two hours of driving."

"I don't have a car."

"I do, and I'll come down every weekend."

"Don't you have a magician's meeting this Saturday?"

"Yeah, but that's not till evening. I'll drive down in the morning."

"And miss sleeping in?" I teased. Josh was *not* a morning person.

"Hey, it's a sacrifice I'm willing to make for you. So stop looking so worried. Distance is not going to change anything."

I was relieved Josh wasn't upset . . . yet disappointed, too. Why did he have to be so calm and understanding? Couldn't he complain just a little?

By lunchtime, word of my leaving had spread all over school (most likely via Penny-Love) and while I was sitting at my usual table with the cheerleaders, kids I knew and some I didn't know came over. Most acted upbeat and said things like, "You'll have more fun in a big city," "Moving will be an exciting change," or "You'll make new friends."

Instead of being reassured, fear mounted. I didn't want new friends, and I didn't want to even think about my old friends. The ones I left behind when I fled six months ago. How could I go back to that life? And where would I go to school? Arcadia High was out of the question. My mother couldn't expect me to return there—not after I'd been kicked out. More likely, Mom would enroll me in a private school. Somewhere with boring rules and tacky uniforms.

Just kill me now, please!

Walls closed in and I felt like I could hardly breathe. Making a lame excuse about getting something in my locker, I jumped up from the table and fled to the computer lab where Manny DeVries could always be found working on the latest issue of the school newspaper, *Sheridan Shout-Out*.

Instead of his usual grin, Manny scowled at me and demanded, "Is it true?"

"So you've heard already." Wearily, I sank into a chair beside his computer console. "Bad news travels fast."

"I won't act like I'm okay with this, because I'm not. How can someone as smart as you do something so dumb?"

With a heavy sigh, I explained about my mother's verdict.

When I finished, Manny narrowed his dark eyes, resembling a punk pirate with dreads snagged in a ponytail and a gold eyebrow ring. "Drastic measures are required. Don't make me kidnap you."

"One kidnapping is all you're allowed. And you used your quota up last week when you and Thorn put me under house arrest."

"Classic moment," he said proudly. "Speaking of Thorn, have you told her yet?"

I bit my lip and shook my head. Thorn and I had a prickly enough friendship. She was a chain-wearing, black-garbed Goth with an anti-social attitude, while I hung out with cheerleaders. When Manny introduced us, it was dislike at first sight. But when I found out Thorn had a psychic ability, too—psychometry—I was intrigued. We got to know each other better on a road trip, learning mutual respect. Still, Thorn was quick-tempered with unpredictable moods and I had no idea how she'd react to my leaving. Maybe I'd send her an email or write a letter.

Manny gave me a stern look, as if reading my mind. "Seriously, Beany," he added, "leaving is a lose-lose situation. The newspaper needs you."

"You'll find another proofreader."

"But no one with your *special* talents."

I smiled sadly. He may have a reputation of being a player, but he'd been a real friend to me. He kept my secrets and in return I helped with his Mystic Manny column by giving him authentic predictions. I foretold hook-ups, heartbreaks, and what students would be doing in ten years. Manny's readers were amazed with his uncanny accuracy.

"You have special talents, too," I pointed out. "You've helped Dominic and I track down info on my ancestors and the missing charms. You're an amazing researcher."

"Go on, say more. I thrive on compliments."

"Watch out, your head is swelling."

"Is that all?" He glanced down with a wicked grin.

"You are so bad."

"Stick around and I'll show you how bad I can be."

"Save it for your girlfriends."

"So many girls, only one Manny," he joked.

"Egotist!" I swatted his arm.

"Just telling it like it is. Some guys have it, and some guys have more of it."

"More than I need to know." I gave a bittersweet smile, thinking how much I'd miss teasing with him. "Anyway, don't worry about predictions for your column. I'll email them from San Jose."

"Thanks, but it won't be the same." His expression sobered. "Will you be going back to your old school?"

"No!" I said a bit too sharply. "I could never return there after all the lies and accusations. I'd rather die."

As I said the word "die," a chill shivered through me. I grabbed tight to my chair as dizziness struck. Lights flickered around the classroom, bright colors spinning into confusing images. Posters fluttered like birds in flight and white walls shimmered into a silver sandstorm.

I stood swaying, afraid of passing out. To clear my head, I focused on the floor. Only the tile whirled, changing from dull-gray squares to golden polished wood. The computer lab was gone, replaced with a silvery cave. And Manny had vanished.

But I wasn't alone. Ghostly white-clothed figures glided around me on the golden floor, shifting in quick moves like living chess pieces. They had no faces, only blurry gray masks. With deft spins, they paired and began battling among themselves, slashing with blade-shaped arms and razor claw fingers. They ignored me, except for one. A lone figure glided toward me, slowly, with chilling purpose, gleaming silver claws outstretched. I was paralyzed, unable to move, watching in terror as knife claws loomed closer, closer . . .

"Sabine . . . Beany!" Manny snapped his fingers in front of my face.

"Huh?" I jumped back to reality; the hum of computers, the bright lights overhead and posters on faded white walls.

"You're so pale," Manny said, leaning closer and studying me. "Did something just happen? Was it a vision?"

"Yeah . . . I think so." I clasped my hands in my lap to keep from shaking.

"Tell me," he insisted.

So I did. And when I finished, he stared at me with both concern and curiosity. "Knives, figures in white, a chess board? Any idea what it means?" he asked.

"No." I shook my head numbly. "But it could be a warning."

"A warning for whom?"

"I don't know, but I have a bad feeling." I shuddered. "If I don't find out, something terrible will happen."

4

My suitcase bulged, a red shirt hanging out like a distress signal. Tucking the shirt back in, I shoved down hard on the lid, then grabbed the metal zipper tag. Ziiip! A sound so final my heart nearly broke.

Soon my mother would arrive to take me away.

My gaze drifted to my window, a view I loved dearly, and I thought how very far away the tree-tops seemed. I hadn't even left, yet I was already homesick. It felt like I was being split apart; my body moving to San Jose while my heart stayed in Sheridan Valley.

The floor shook when I heaved my bulky suitcase off my bed. A card that had been propped on my dresser fluttered to the carpet. Picking it up, I smiled sadly at Penny-Love's computer graphics of a redheaded cheerleader waving poms and doing the split in midair with a caption that read, "Gimme a G—O—O—D—B—Y—E!"

"Nothing good about goodbye," I grumbled.

Never overlook a silver lining, a woman's voice snapped in my head.

"Opal?" I shut my eyes to connect more clearly with my spirit guide, and had a vague sense of her upswept hair, ageless tawny skin, and critical dark eyes.

Your behavior brings me considerable disappointment. Are you finished wallowing in your pity party?

"I'd rather wallow at Nona's All Hallows party. I'll miss out on all the fun tonight. I have a right to be unhappy."

Frankly my girl, you've extended your self-indulgence quota by a marathon mile. Abandon negative energy and focus on the positive.

"My life is very un-positive," I retorted, colors crystallizing into shapes until I could clearly see Opal, looking regal in a flowing, jeweled, ivory caftan.

Your melancholy view is quite unbecoming and unnecessary. What may seem like a dark night is not without a guiding light.

"How can you say that? Everything is messed up. I'm being forced to leave my sick grandmother, the most perfect boyfriend I'll ever have, and great friends. They're all annoyingly understanding, except for Thorn. She's taking it personally and won't even talk to me."

Emotions are deliciously complicated, aren't they? Rather than focus on the negative, I suggest you evaluate the positive aspects of your life.

"There aren't any."

On the contrary, you possess abundant blessings that blindly go unnoticed. I challenge you to find three things good about this pending move.

"Three? You might as well ask for a million."

Sa . . . bine! Her voice crackled with disapproval and warning.

"Oh, all right, I'll try." I sank on my bed and thought hard. "I suppose it's good that I'll be able to see more of my sisters. Amy keeps emailing me about all the things she wants to do together. Even Ashley sounded excited in her last phone call. I'm glad I'll be able to celebrate Halloween with them. It was always our favorite holiday and we have special traditions, like making caramel popcorn and watching old black-and-white horror films. The twins are growing up so fast and I think we need each other."

Excellent observation, and more true than you realize. They are not the only ones who will benefit by your move. And what else?

"The weather is more comfortable in San Jose."

I'm sure you can do better than that. Have you no feelings for your parents?

"I suppose it'll be nice to see more of Dad. But Amy tells me he's working so much, he's hardly ever home."

What about your mother?

"Oh, her. She's ruining my life."

Your life is far from ruined. On the contrary, you are a sun in your universe, and radiate a strong influence to those around you. So listen with your heart. To move forward, you must circle back and heal old wounds.

"Huh?" I groaned. "English please."

Moments that seem lost to the past are actually turns of destiny waiting to be revealed. There is a wrong you have the opportunity to set right and much will be discovered along this journey.

I shook my head, sinking deeper in confusion. "Does this have something to do with my vision of figures in white with knife-fingers?"

Glimpses of the future are protective armor preparing you for a battle.

"But I don't want to battle anyone. Can't you just tell me what's going on so I can deal with it now?"

Answers can be found in your dreams.

"Dreams?" I repeated, completely frustrated. "I hate my dreams! Even since the accident, I've slept badly and can't even remember my dreams."

The result of an unwillingness to face the messenger.

"What messenger?"

The spirit who visits in the night. Be assured, you have nothing to fear from him, as he only seeks your help.

"A visitor in the night? Seeking help?"

In a shock of memory, it all rushed back. The dream that wasn't a dream at all, but a visitation from a spirit in a #17 football jersey. Kip Hurst! "Help her," that's what he asked. But I couldn't remember anything else.

Why had Kip come to me anyway? I should be the last person he'd contact. I hadn't been able to help him and he'd died. How could he expect me to help someone else? Especially when he didn't tell me who needed help.

Was this unknown girl a stranger?

Or someone I already knew?

5

My mother was late.

I kept checking through the living room window, pacing a path on the carpet, and growing more anxious as seconds passed. I even walked outside and peered down our long driveway, but no sign of any cars.

As I started back into the house, I heard someone call out, "Sabine! Wait!"

Turning on the porch steps, I saw Dominic rushing toward me. His sandy brown hair flew back from his tanned face and I found myself thinking how good he looked in his faded jeans. My traitorous heart sped up.

"Hey," I said, a bit shyly.

"Good. You're still here." He shoved his hands in his pockets, facing me with a closed expression. A guy of few words, it was impossible to know what he was thinking, although I couldn't help but wonder.

"Mom is late, and that's not like her so I should probably call her cell and find out when she'll be here or if something is wrong." I had this dumb habit of rambling when I got nervous. And with Dominic, I was always nervous.

"Stuck in traffic," he guessed.

"That must be it. I'm sure she'll show up soon. Not that I'm in a hurry. Maybe she'll cancel and I can postpone leaving for a day. Then I'll be here to celebrate Halloween at Nona's party."

"Nona wanted to have it early for you."

"I know, but I wouldn't let her. A lot of her clients and friends already RVSPed. Everyone will have a wonderful party," I added sadly.

"Not everyone."

I wondered if he was talking about himself. He was gazing at me so strangely, I was afraid to say anything; there were words better left unsaid between us. So I babbled on, "I tried convincing Mom to delay my move home, but she insisted this morning was the only free time in her schedule to pick me up."

"I could have taken you if I still had my truck."

"Your poor truck. I'm so sorry." I winced. Dominic wouldn't have been driving that night if not for me. And now his truck was ruined.

"Not your fault. I shouldn't have swerved."

"And smacked into that cow? I don't think so! Swerving probably saved us both—and the cow."

He grinned ruefully. "Maybe."

We just stood there, the way he was staring at me made me self-conscious. I hadn't slept well and knew I looked a mess. I should have used some makeup or parted my hair to the side so it covered the nasty bruise on my cheek.

"I—I should go inside and call Mom . . ."

I started to turn, but he reached out for my hand. When his fingers touched my skin, electricity surged through me. I felt weak and warm and scared all at once.

"Wait," he spoke quietly. "I have to tell you something."

"What?" Our eyes met and I could barely think. I wanted to ask him so many things. Like why he was looking at me that way and if those kisses we shared were accidental or meant anything.

He started to reply, but a bird shrieked overhead, making us both jump. Whatever spell we'd been under broke. He glanced skyward and I followed his gaze to where a shadowy falcon circled.

"Is that Dagger?" I stepped away from Dominic.

"Yep." He nodded. "He's hunting for his breakfast."

"Mice and snakes." I made a sour face. "Yuck."

"Not to Dagger. He loves fresh meat."

"Did he tell you that?"

"He tells me many things," Dominic said mysteriously. He had this uncanny ability to understand animals; they trusted him and he trusted them. He didn't seem to need people, yet I sensed he was interested in me. And I wondered what he'd been about to tell me earlier. That he didn't want me to leave? Or did he even care? Not that I cared if he cared . . . or did I?

Why did he make me so crazy? Putting distance between us was a good idea. Something else to add to Opal's "positive things about the move" list.

"I should go inside," I told him.

"Not yet." He withdrew an envelope from his pocket. His callused fingers brushed against my skin as he placed the bag in my hand. "For you."

"Me?" My voice came out breathless. Had he written something personal? Like a love letter. "You didn't have to . . ."

"Open it."

I slit open the tab with my thumbnail, my hand quivering a bit as I lifted out a small sheet of paper. I didn't recognize the name or Nevada address written down, but I recognized the possibilities. "Is this what I think it is?" I exclaimed.

"Depends what you think."

"The location of the fourth missing charm?"

The corners of his mouth tipped in a smile. "Not missing for long."

"Ohmygod! This is like a miracle!"

"You like it?"

"More than like. This is so incredible! When Manny hears, he's going to want to go right to Nevada."

"I need to check out details first."

"Sure. I can't believe we're so close to having all four charms! How did you find it? Tell me everything!"

"Not much to tell. I checked records of the jeweler who found the third charm and traced information back to one of your ancestors."

My fingers shook as I held the paper. Not a love letter (which I really couldn't handle anyway) but information that touched my heart. "How did you finally get this address?"

"From an old phone book. But the info could be outdated, so I have to make some more calls."

"I wonder what the fourth charm will be."

"We'll know soon."

I gazed at him, full of gratitude and so much more. Now we had charms of a cat, a house, and a fish. Once we found the fourth charm, we'd have all the puzzle pieces. But would these old clues be enough to reveal the secret location of the missing remedy book? Could a book still be intact after over a hundred years? It had to be. It was the only hope for Nona.

"You're frowning," Dominic said quietly.

"I'm just worried about Nona. And I have to leave so I won't be here for her."

"I will be."

"But for how long? You'll find a better job when you finish learning how to be a horse shoer."

"A farrier," he corrected.

"Whatever. You're too smart to just do handyman work and you'll move on."

"Not until Nona is well. Promise."

His tone was so sincere my heart ached. Staring into his blue eyes was like diving into an unfathomable ocean. I could hardly think and forgot how to breathe. Sinking deep, down, down . . .

Remember Josh, I told myself. Sweet honest Josh who would never, ever cheat on you. Your boyfriend.

Sanity returned, accompanied by shame and guilt.

There was a rumbling in the distance and I saw my mother's car turning in at the gate. "I have to go," I said quickly.

"Can I help you with your suitcase?" Dominic offered.

But I shook my head firmly. "I can manage."

"If you ever need anything—anything at all—just ask."

"I'll remember that." I slipped the address back in the envelope and slipped it in my pocket. "Let me know what else you learn. Nona is counting on us to figure this out."

"We will." He paused and added, "Partner."

"Yeah . . . partners."

We stepped apart as my mother's car came to a stop in front of the house.

"And Sabine?" he called out softly.

"What?"

"I'll miss you." Then he turned and walked away.

6

A goblin, a skeleton, and two tiny Ewoks held out bags and chanted "Trick or Treat!"

Oh, joy! I'd traded Nona's wonderful All Hallow's party for door duty with miniature candy grabbers.

Elegant pumpkin lanterns glowed along the paved pathway to the porch where mechanical witches whirled overhead on glowing broomsticks.

An interior decorator had transformed the house with lacy cobwebs and tasteful porcelain Halloween figurines. My family was famous throughout the neighborhood for having the best decorations and designer goodie bags.

My father usually manned the door in a Dracula or Frankenstein costume. He would joke that a monster costume was more comfortable than his business suits. He didn't have time for joking these days, but he had planned to stay home Halloween night—until at the last minute his assistant called. With apologies, he'd rushed off for an important meeting.

Mom was committed to chaperoning the masquerade party for my sisters' dance class, and my sisters were decked out in wicked costumes. I had planned to go along, too, so I could be with my sisters. But now someone had to stay behind.

Guess who?

As I handed out goodie bags (decorative bags crammed with giant candy bars and toy surprises), I wistfully thought of Sheridan Valley.

Nona's party would start soon.

Her farm was too rural for trick-or-treaters, but it was spookily perfect for an All Hallows party.

Guests would be greeted by carved candle-lit pumpkins glowing from the windows and Mr. and Mrs. Scarecrow waving from their cozy perch on the porch rail. I'd helped make the scarecrow couple, collecting straw from the barn and stuffing it into an old dress of Nona's and a pair of Grady's overalls. Grady was Nona's poker pal and he'd joked about the special dish he was bringing to the All Hallows party. "I call it haunted chili because it has a second life."

Nona's friend Velvet was bringing desserts from her chocolate/New Age shop. After everyone filled up on sinfully delicious truffles and candy apples, Velvet and Nona would give tarot readings. I wasn't skilled in the art of tarot, but Velvet had given me a book on palm reading and I'd planned to try it out at the party.

I glanced at the phone, tempted to call and see how things were going . . . but resisted. It was better to make a clean break.

Another doorbell chime.

Dutifully, I rose from the couch and went to the door.

"Treat-Treat!" a tiny faery chirped, waving a wand in her chubby toddler fingers. Her beaming mother chuckled and held out a cloth sack.

I knelt down, grinned at the cute little girl, then plopped in a goodie bag. Mother and faery thanked me, then scampered off to the next house. Shutting the door, I settled back on the couch to watch reruns of Bewitched on cable.

Samantha's mother was just about to cast a spell on Darren when the doorbell chimed again. A huge group screamed "trick or treat" and eager hands waved pillowcases, hollowed plastic pumpkins, and plastic grocery bags. By the time I got back, the show was over. I clicked off the TV just as the chimes rang out again.

"What is this? Grand Center Halloween?" I muttered, heading for the door.

The Three Musketeers stood on the doorstep. Two short swashbucklers and the third was an adult who towered at least a foot over me; clearly a father getting into the fun of the evening. The little kids, a boy and girl, waved plastic swords, while their father carried a rounded-tip saber. I had one just like it when I took fencing classes.

In fact, the adult looked familiar. He was all sharp angles and skinny, with tight, brown curly hair, a prominent curved nose, and a goatee.

"Mr. Landreth!" I exclaimed, bumping into the tray and knocking several bags to the floor. I stared in shock at my ex-fencing teacher. "Is it really you?"

"Have we met?" He sounded puzzled, then looked closer. Surprise lit up his face. "Sabine? My goodness, it is you. But I thought you moved away."

"I just moved back."

"That's wonderful!" He tucked his foil at his side. "It's great to see you again."

"You, too. And these must be your kids?"

"Timothy and Lismari. Or for tonight Aramis and Porthos," he added, fondly patting their heads.

"I'm Aramis," the little girl said proudly. "The bestest musky-teer."

"I'm the bravest, Porthos," her brother put in.

"And I'm Sabine," I told them with a smile.

"Milady Sabine?" Little Aramis asked.

"Huh?" I said.

Mr. Landreth glanced fondly at his daughter. "She means the villainess from the Three Muska-teers movie. The lethally beautiful Milady Sabine de Winter."

"She's really bad and gets her head chopped off," his son added with a wave of his plastic sword.

"Should I be afraid?" I joked.

My ex-teacher chuckled. "You're safe, but I'm not sure about myself with these mini swash-bucklers."

"I can't believe you're a dad," I told my ex-teacher as I handed each child a goodie bag. "You always seemed like a big kid yourself."

"Guilty as charged. What better job than playing with swords? You were one of my most skilled students. I hated losing you."

"Well . . . it was a difficult time."

"None of it your fault," he said firmly. "The whole school was struck by mass hysteria."

"Except you," I said gratefully. Mr. Landreth had been the only teacher who stuck up for me. I'd heard that he had a shouting match with the principal, calling him an idiot for blaming me for Kip's death. My teacher even threatened to quit his job. Fortunately that didn't happen.

"It's so great you're back." Mr. Landreth smiled. "Don't forget to sign up for my advanced class."

"I won't be going to Arcadia High."

"Oh? Too bad, although it's understandable. Where will you go?"

"I'm not sure. Probably a private school."

"I recommend Saint Marks. They have a solid fencing program. Talent like yours shouldn't be wasted."

"Thanks," I said, blushing. I wasn't used to praise and wasn't sure how to reply.

"I mean it, Sabine," he added sincerely. "Have you kept up on your fencing?"

"No," I admitted. I could have explained that Sheridan High didn't offer fencing, but that was only part of the reason.

"You can't be serious!" he exclaimed. "You need to get back in—"

"Daddy, we wanna go to more houses," Lismari interrupted, tugging on his arm. "Come on, Dad," Timothy added.

"Just a minute," he told them. Then he gave me an earnest look. "Sabine, you can't neglect your skills. We have to talk about this more."

"I'm not that interested in fencing."

"I don't believe it. You had a real passion for the sport. I know that upsetting things happened at

Arcadia, and I'm ashamed at the behavior of some of my colleagues and your teammates. If you'd continued you could be competing nationally by now."

I glanced down at the candy dish, shutting out memories. "I've moved on," I told him simply. "It's over."

"It doesn't have to be." Mr. Landreth reached in his pocket and pulled out a business card. "Take this, Sabine. In addition to working at Arcadia, I'm also teaching fencing classes at the Learning Express. I'll give you private lessons."

"I'm not interested."

"Just think about it."

I shook my head. "I'm through with fencing."

"But fencing isn't through with you." He reached out, opened my palm and placed his card inside. Then his kids pulled him away and the door shut with a soft thud.

Biting my lip, I looked down at the card in my hand. The tiny outline of a sword cut to my heart, and I realized Mr. Landreth was right. I *had* missed fencing. My fingers closed around the card, imagining the firm feel of a sword hilt in my hand. But I couldn't get involved. Not after all the hurt and betrayal.

I shoved the card in my pocket and went back to the couch.

When the chimes rang a minute later, I handed out goodie bags to two fanged monsters, a princess, and a Spiderman with two missing front teeth. The little ghoulies kept coming for another hour. When the chimes finally quieted, I fell asleep on the couch.

I awoke to the sound of the door opening and a burst of voices.

Lifting my head, I saw my sisters laughing as they entered the house. They were both still in costume; Sherlock "Amy" Holmes with a pipe and magnifying glass and Ashley as a punk rocker with spiked purple hair. They were willowy and tall, looking much older than ten. This was the first year the twins didn't wear matching costumes, which made me a little sad.

"You missed the most amazing party!" Ashley exclaimed, bouncing on the couch by me and waving her jeweled guitar in the air.

"Astute deduction, my dear Ashley," Amy said, puffing on her toy pipe and blowing soap bubbles.

"I'm glad you had fun." I sat up and yawned.

"Mom stayed behind to clean up and discuss some boring committee," Amy told me. "Leanna's dad dropped us off."

She gestured behind her and that's when I noticed a slightly overweight man with his arm around a slender girl in a cat costume. Short, dark curls framed Leanna's large, night-black eyes. The young girl didn't smile, but hung back shyly.

Or was it more than shyness? I caught an odd look exchanged between my sisters and sensed that something was going on I didn't understand. I waited for them to introduce me, but instead they turned abruptly away.

"Thanks for the ride," Ashley said to Leanna's father.

"No problem," he said. "Your mother does so much for the kids, it's the least I can do."

"Thanks and happy Halloween," Amy said in a too-cheerful tone. Something was definitely going on. I felt shut out and hurt that my sisters were either too ashamed or embarrassed to introduce me.

Leanna's hand was poised on the door as if she was eager to escape. Her gaze shifted in my direction, wide-eyed and tight-lipped. She looked terrified.

Of me?

I offered her a smile, hoping to show I was harmless. Only she didn't smile back. And as I watched, a glowing shape appeared over her dark curls. Round, pale with dark eyes, a nose and mouth.

A disembodied head—Kip Hurst!

Kip winked at me, then floated like a ghostly balloon so he was face-to-face with Leanna. I wanted to shout at him to get away from her. Instead, my hand flew over my mouth or I would have gasped as Leanna's human face and Kip's ghostly face blended together like a double-exposed photograph.

They looked uncannily alike; similar dark eyes, rounded chins, and dark brown curly hair. And I realized something astonishing. No wonder Leanna's name sounded familiar. She was the reason my mother hadn't wanted me to attend my sisters' tenth birthday party. My mother feared my presence would upset Leanna.

I knew why Kip had appeared—even more importantly—why he was hovering by Leanna. He was Leanna's brother.

7

My hand slipped from my mouth and I cried out.

All heads turned toward me, including the disembodied one smirking with ghostly amusement.

"What is it, Sabine?" Amy asked anxiously.

"I—I . . . saw . . . a—"

My heart raced, but I realized I must look and sound like a crazy person. But I couldn't exactly blurt out to Leanna, "I saw your brother's head."

The last thing I needed was to start new rumors about my weird abilities. Besides, it was obvious no one else could see Kip.

"What is it, Sabine?" Amy persisted.

"Nothing."

"But something startled you."

Kip had his mouth open in a silent laugh— the dead jerk. How dare he think this was funny? Well I wouldn't let him make a fool of me.

"I saw a spider," I lied.

"Where?" Ashley cried out in alarm, looking around. "Is it near me?"

"No, it was crawling on my arm."

"Ooh, gross. I hate spiders."

"Me, too." I nodded at Ashley. "They freak me out."

"Since when?" Amy asked suspiciously. She knew me too well, and probably remembered the pet spider I'd named Charlie.

I brushed my hand across my forearm. "It's gone now."

And so was Kip. Thank goodness! If he showed up again, I'd have to have a serious girl-to-ghost talk and tell him firmly to stay away.

Before Amy could ask any more questions, I faked a yawn and said I was going to bed. Once in my room, I sank wearily on my bed.

What a night! Moving back home had been a mistake.

Like old Ebeneezer, I was being haunted by ghosts of the past. Not-so-dearly-departed Kip wanted my help, my ex-teacher wanted to help me, and my very presence had terrified a young girl. I hadn't even been back a full day and the past was dragging me down like an heavy chains, tightening its grip around me.

I glanced over at my suitcase, still unpacked, and wished I had the courage to leave before it was too late.

Or was it already too late?

I could understand Leanna disliking me, but her terror was beyond normal. Why would she be afraid of me? Did she think I was into black magic or part of a satanic cult? Did she believe all the exaggerated rumors about me after her brother died? Did she think I caused his death?

Or maybe her fear was about something else entirely. Kip had asked me to help an unknown girl. Did he mean Leanna? Was she in some kind of trouble?

My sisters would know. I could count on Amy to tell me anything, but I wasn't so sure about Ashley. Would she be more loyal to her friend or her big sister? I was afraid to find out.

Before moving in with Nona, I'd been close to both of my sisters. More of a second mother since Mom was busy with society commitments and scheduling the twins' singing and dancing lessons. Unfortunately, Mom never scheduled any "fun" time. So I took the girls to movies, played games, and had gossip sessions in our tree house. But when I moved out, we drifted apart.

Sighing, I sat up on my bed, catching my reflection in my dresser mirror. I still looked the same: green eyes, slim shape (not enough shape up top, much to my dismay), and long blond hair with a black streak. The black mark of a seer seemed darker and wider; a dividing line separating me from my family. And I longed for the easy friendship I used to have with my sisters.

Past Halloweens the three of us celebrated our traditional "Homemade Halloween." After movies and popcorn, we'd gather in my room and exchange Halloween gifts. This secret exchange started a few years ago when I found a vintage copy of Nancy Drew, *The Sign of the Twisted Candles,* at a yard sale and gave it to Amy on Halloween. Ashley wanted to know if I had a gift for her, too.

Thinking fast, I went into my room, found a ball of rainbow colored yarn and quickly crocheted a chain bracelet. To my surprise, Ashley loved the simple bracelet. On the next Halloween, the girls wanted to exchange gifts again. I agreed but added a rule that only "homemade" gifts were allowed and it had to be a secret.

Of course this year, the tradition was over.

There was a tap at my door. It was Amy.

"So what made you gasp?" Amy demanded as she plopped beside me on the bed.

"I told you—I saw a spider."

"Since when are you scared of little spiders?"

"It wasn't little, it was huge."

"I didn't see it."

"I swatted it away."

Amy shook her dark head. "You're lying."

"How can you accuse me of such a thing?" I tried to sound outraged.

"I read enough mysteries to know how to tell when someone isn't telling the truth. You didn't meet my eyes and your voice got squeaky. I don't have to be as good as Nancy Drew to know you're hiding something."

"Nancy could learn something from you," I said with a rueful smile.

"I knew you wouldn't panic over a spider. You looked like you saw a ghost."

I paused. "I did."

"Really?" she asked. "So what's the big deal? You're used to seeing ghosts."

"Not a ghost like this," I said with a shiver.

Amy leaned closer, her dark eyes shining. "Tell me all about it."

"All about what?" Ashley cut in, appearing in the doorway; tall and dramatic with her long dark hair frizzed out with purple punk spikes and her face exaggerated with makeup.

"Sabine didn't see a spider," Amy explained.

"I knew she was lying." Ashley came over to stand beside my bed. "You're not a very good liar."

"Gee, thanks," I said sarcastically.

"Sabine was going to tell me about the ghost she saw. I can't wait to hear all about it."

"Not me," Ashley said in a disapproving tone that reminded me of Mom. "Keep your ghosts to yourself, thank you very much. It's just too . . . unnatural."

"You're jealous because Sabine is psychic and you're not."

"Like I'd want everyone to think I'm a freak? No way."

"Sabine is not a freak, and you're mean to say that."

"I didn't say she was, I just said I didn't want to be."

"Which is the same thing," Amy cried, jumping up and glaring at her twin. "I can't believe we're related."

"I wish we weren't."

"And I wish you were—"

"Time out!" Before this war turned bloody, I gestured for them to stop. "Hey, you never told me about your party. How did it go?"

Amy glowered, but Ashley perked up. "Oh, the party. It was way cool. I won a prize for Best Crazy Hair."

"Congrats!" I said, relieved to talk about something safe. Ashley launched into a vivid description of the games (pin the nose on the wicked witch and a tossing game with skull bean bags). Amy joined in, and soon we were giggling together.

Then Ashley gave Amy what I'd always called the "twin look;" sharing their own special wavelength. A psychic channel I'd never been able to read.

They said they'd be right back, then hurried out of the room. I had no idea what was going on—until they returned, each holding a small wrapped gift.

"Happy Halloween!" they rang out.

"Our tradition!" I cried in surprise. "I didn't think you'd remember."

"How could we forget?" Ashley grinned. "And I followed the rules."

"Me, too," Amy said. "Only homemade gifts—nothing from a store."

"We already exchanged our own gifts with each other. Before we found out you'd be here, we agreed to give each other Creative Coupons."

"My idea," Ashley said proudly. "I made Amy coupons for stuff like taking out the garbage, doing dishes, and foot massages."

"I made coupons to clean her room, homework help, and reading aloud from our favorite books. But we kept our gifts to you a secret, even from each other."

I stared at them, warmed inside. Maybe we'd drifted apart, but shared memories and moments like this brought us back together.

"I didn't expect anything. You girls are just so . . . so amazing."

"We know that," Ashley said with a laugh. "Now would you open your gifts already. Mine first."

"But I didn't even know I was going to be here soon enough to make anything. I feel awful because I don't have gifts for you."

"You already gave us something great," Amy insisted.

"Yeah," Ashley nodded. "You're here."

They shared a twin look and said, "You're our gift."

8

The next morning I tacked Amy's gift on the wall over my desk; a penciled sketch of Nona's farmhouse with Lilybelle playfully swatting a cow's tale. Amy must have known how much I'd miss living with Nona. Ashley had made a creative gift, too. She'd combined her singing and song-writing skills into a personalized recording of original songs sung by her.

And that wasn't the end of our traditional Halloween celebration.

My sisters sorted through horror movies while I headed for the kitchen to make caramel popcorn. Caramels were melting on the stove when I heard the door creak and glanced over to see Amy.

"We need to talk alone," she explained. Then she sniffed the pan. "Hmm, smells yummy."

"Watch out, the pan is hot. So what's up?"

"That's what I want to know. Ashley is busy sorting through movies, so you can tell me the truth," she said in a low voice. "About the ghost you saw."

"I only saw his head."

"Ooh, creepy. Was the head all bloody?"

"No. But he freaked me out for other reasons." I glanced at the door to make sure it was closed so Ashley wouldn't hear. "It was Kip."

"You mean . . . Kip Hurst?" Her eyes bugged out. "Leanna's brother?"

"That's the dead guy. I think he wants me to help Leanna."

"Why? She doesn't need help. Leanna has a starring solo in our dance recital and she's really popular because she does nice stuff like bringing treats when it's not even anyone's birthday."

"Does she have any problems?"

"I don't think so. She's like the luckiest person I know."

"Except she lost her brother," I reminded gravely. "How's she handling that?"

"Okay, I guess. She never talks about him."

"But she was afraid of me. Any idea why?"

"Well, yeah." Amy glanced down at the bubbling caramel on the stove. "But don't get mad."

"Mad? About what?"

"Leanna thinks you can do black magic. She's afraid you'll hex her."

"Hex her?" I stared at her, dumbfounded. "You've got to be kidding."

"She's watched way too many reruns of Charmed. Besides, she's Ashley's best friend, not mine," Amy added as if that explained everything.

"Did Ashley tell her I wasn't a witch?"

"Yeah, but Leanna's so stubborn. Like even though Ashley keeps bugging her, she won't hold a sleepover at her house."

"Why not?"

"She says her bedroom is too small. But I wouldn't know cause I've never seen it. She never invites anyone over—not even Ashley."

I turned off the stove. Instead of reaching for the pan, I stared in surprise at my sister. "Her best friend hasn't been to her house?"

"Leanna says she likes ours better."

"Doesn't that seem strange to you?"

"I never wanted to go there anyway."

"But she must have a reason for not inviting her friends over."

"Like a secret? By jove, you could be right," Amy pulled out her toy Sherlock Holmes pipe and tapped it against the kitchen counter. "Astounding observation, my dear sister. Like this book I read where a girl's parents were kidnapped and the bad guys moved in with her and she had to act like everything was okay. But her identical cousin found out and traded places with her and the villains were caught."

I chuckled. "I doubt Leanna is hiding anything that wild."

"But if she has a secret, I'm going to find out."

"I can always count on you."

"I'll send you a bill," she joked. Then we carried sodas and caramel popcorn into the family room.

By the time I went to bed that night, I was exhausted in a good way. I sorted through my box of night-lights until I found one shaped like a musical note that Amy had given me.

I awoke feeling refreshed and eager, at first not sure why I was in such a good mood. Then I remembered.

Josh was coming this morning!

I couldn't wait to see him. We'll have the whole wonderful day together. But what would we do? Hanging out at my house could get boring. I'd have to think of somewhere else to go. My old hangouts like West Valley Mall or the ice skating rink were out of the question. What if I ran into someone I knew from Arcadia High? Seriously awkward.

Josh knew I'd been forced out of my old school, but he didn't know the whole story. His best pal (and my worst enemy) Evan Marshall tried to turn Josh against me by telling him that I'd predicted Kip's death. Only Evan's plan backfired. Josh was outraged that I'd been accused of having supernatural powers. He thought my dad should have sued my accusers for slander. And he'd warned Evan not to spread any rumors about me at Sheridan High.

I loved how Josh wanted to protect my reputation . . . but did I love *him*?

Doubts kept creeping in, especially when Dominic was around. So today would be all about me and Josh. We could do something romantic, like picnic by a lake or drive to the Overlook where there was this amazing view of the city. Not once would I think of Dominic.

After quickly slipping into jeans and a stretchy sky blue top, I went to the kitchen, popped a frozen waffle in the toaster, and poured orange juice. No one else was up, so the house was eerily still; the only sounds from the hum of the refrigerator and the ticking of a wall clock.

It was strange to be back here; sorting through a cupboard for cereal, pouring non-fat milk (the only kind Mom would buy), sitting alone at the kitchen nook by the large picture window. I stared at familiar things and felt out of place. Like I was a visitor in someone else's life.

It was too early for Josh to arrive, so after washing my dishes (house rules); I returned to my room to check email. Two from Penny-Love, a joke from

Manny, and over a dozen spam. But nothing from Josh. He was probably already on his way.

So I listened to Ashley's songs, her sweet raspy voice making me feel less alone. I pulled out my craft bag, sorted through yarn and fabric, and worked on a knitted scarf for Nona. A magazine article I'd read said that knitting was creative meditating. I agreed. My fingers moved swiftly and automatically. Clink, ping, clink, ping. The silver clash of needles was mesmerizing. Thrust and parry, metal striking then retreating, then striking again, like a miniature sword battle.

And I thought of fencing.

It had been so cool to see Mr. Landreth again, but unsettling, too. He'd said fencing wasn't finished with me. But what did he know? I hadn't fenced in over six months and survived just fine. Fencing was over for me and I was okay with that.

Or was I?

Fencing always gave me such a huge rush—suiting up in protective clothes, wielding a saber, and facing an opponent. My competitive fire ignited, and I felt like a warrior going into battle. Nothing else existed except my opponent and me. Sometimes when it was over, I'd look up to find spectators applauding.

What an honor when I received the invitation to join Foils! I'd grinned for days. The elite exhibition group only included the most skilled teen fencers and was locally famous for performing demonstrations at mall openings, fairs, and other special events. I still had my shirt with the silver sword design below the word Foils and the matching silver pants. I'd loved being in Foils. Not because of the performing (I was a little shy about that part), but because of the tight friendships. Foils became my second family, and a group of us always hung out at school: Tony, Jennae, Derrick, Alphonso, Tiffany, Vin, and Brianne.

Brianne. My ex-best friend.

Needles slipped, and a sharp point stabbed my thumb.

Why did I have to go think of her? Bold, impulsive, betraying Brianne. We'd been inseparable since third grade when she moved across the street. We made up a fantasy world called "Castle Kingdom" with cardboard boxes and stick swords. Petite Brianne looked like exquisite porcelain, yet always took the role of the bold knight who rescued the captured princess (me) from a horrible dungeon.

She was fearless, while things like loud voices and darkness scared me. But at sleepovers, I was the one who scared her by telling ghost stories. I'd been surprised to find out she didn't see ghosts or even know the name of her spirit guide (Septina, a wise Egyptian woman). And when I tried to explain about the other side, she thought I was making it up. She eventually believed me and we bonded like sisters—until she changed. I still didn't know why. But with a stroke of a pen, she turned against me, signing a petition to kick me out of school.

Her betrayal cut me deeper than a thousand swords.

A ringing phone startled me and I jumped, scattering knitting needles and yarn to the carpet. By the time I reached the hall phone, the ringing had stopped. Then my mother's bedroom door opened and she came out in a robe, her hair mussed, and wearing an annoyed expression instead of makeup. She didn't say anything as she handed me the phone, but her frown warned that it was too early for phone calls on a Saturday.

"Thanks," I murmured, then I grabbed the phone and retreated to my room.

It was Josh—with bad news.

9

I didn't yell or complain or smash the phone into a million pieces.

Although I wanted to.

Instead I assured Josh I understood he couldn't refuse a lunch invitation from his mentor in magic, The Amazing Arturo. Of course I didn't mind that he was busy on Sunday, too. We'd see each other next weekend. He should have a wonderful time and not worry about me.

If Ashley heard me, she'd take back what she said about my being a terrible liar.

I was damn good at lying.

And heartbroken.

But what would it solve to lose my temper? Josh would be disappointed in me and I'd end up feeling guilty. Even after I slammed down the phone and punched my pillow until it was a squashy lump, I felt awful. I'd counted on having Josh here for support. Now a long, empty day stretched ahead.

If I still lived with Nona, there'd be tons to do. Walking in the woods, hunting for chicken eggs, helping Nona around the house, or catching up on the latest gossip with Penny-Love. Ms. Love Doctor was probably busy working for Nona, while I was stuck here with nothing to do.

Be positive, I could hear Opal in my head.

Okay, okay. It wasn't like I was completely alone. My sisters were just down the hall. I could hang out with them today.

So I went to Amy's room, and tapped on the door.

After Amy called out, "Come in," I stepped inside. She was curled up in a red beanbag by her window, her thick hair spilling around her like a dark cloud. She glanced up from the book she was reading and grinned at me.

"Morning, Sis," she said. "Sleep okay?"

"If you mean, did I see any more ghosts, the answer is no. How about you?"

"Fell asleep reading."

"Typical Amy Bookworm," I teased, pulling up a chair and sitting beside her.

"I'm not a bookworm. Worms are gross."

"Would you rather be a book bug?"

"Maybe a book butterfly. Yeah, that sounds cool." She tilted her head to study me. "So how you dealing with being home?"

"Nona's house was my home."

"But you're happy here, right? I mean, this is your *real* home."

I hesitated. "It's great being with you and Ashley. Hey, maybe we can do something today. Josh was supposed to visit, but he cancelled. Want to go to a movie later? Ashley's invited, too."

"I'd love to . . . but I can't. And neither can Ashley."

"Oh." I acted casual to hide my disappointment. "How come?"

"Saturday's are always busy. Voice lessons, manicures, and hair stylists." She invited me to go along, only I declined.

When Mom found out I didn't have any plans, she cornered me after breakfast with a purposeful glint in her eyes. I caught a whiff of her carnation-scented perfume and was close enough to see faint wrinkles under her carefully made-up face. She wore a tasteful beige suit, camel-colored low heels, and a pearl necklace with matching pearl earrings.

"Sabine, I've been waiting for a quiet moment to have a serious discussion," she said, idly stroking her necklace. "Let's go in the family room and talk privately. We need to make some decisions before Monday."

"About what?" I asked nervously.

"Your schooling."

Panic sliced through me. Here came the big talk about going to a private school with boring uniforms. Or what if it was worse? What if despite everything, Mom wanted me to return to Arcadia High?

But a sudden flash of knowing came to me like a death sentence reprieve.

"Not now, Mom."

"Why not?"

"The phone is going to ring."

"How do you—" she said at the same time the phone rang.

"It's for me," I told her. "I'll get it."

She pursed her lips in a disapproving line. "I hate it when you do that."

Ignoring the acid in her tone, I hurried to answer the phone. And I wasn't even surprised to hear Mr. Landreth's voice. After the first ring, I'd known who was calling. I even knew what he wanted to ask me—if I'd assist with his beginner fencing class this afternoon. He didn't really need an assistant, this was a ploy to get me back into fencing. He hoped once I felt steel in my hand, I'd be hooked and never want to quit.

And I had a feeling he might be right.

When he offered to pick me up, I weighed the risk of falling back in love with my favorite sport against a disturbing talk about school with my mother.

Fencing won. I headed to my closet to dig out my fencing equipment. I lugged out the large oblong bag. Zipping it open, I checked to make sure everything was in there. White canvas protective jacket, saber, epee, foil, steel-mesh helmet, white knickers, and my favorite lavender glove.

An hour later, I was walking into a large gym with wooden floors lined into cross-sectioned strips for fencing.

I felt like I'd come home.

The room even had a distinctive smell, a hint of lemon floor wax and sweat, which might not sound appealing, but I loved it. The air crackled with energy, too, most of it coming from the excited group of beginners lining up against a far wall.

"Everyone, let me introduce my talented assistant Sabine," Mr. Landreth told his class, waving as I joined them.

After a chorus of "Hi Sabine!" I smiled and waved in reply.

There were fifteen fencing students, the ages ranging from guys younger than me to a group of women around Nona's age. This was their second lesson and everyone was excited about using sabers for the first time.

"I can't wait to hit people," a boy with a shaved head and gold earring said.

"Will it hurt?" A middle-aged woman with her auburn hair in a ponytail frowned uneasily.

Mr. Landreth chuckled and tapped his knuckles on his protective helmet. "Nothing gets through this baby. You can smack it all you want and not feel a thing."

"How do we keep score and know who wins?" someone asked.

"In the sport of fencing, the first one to die loses."

A few people looked worried, but then they relaxed when Mr. Landreth chuckled. "No one really dies. It's all very safe," he assured. Then he shifted into teaching mode and announced, "Sabers ready? En garde."

I spent the next hour showing students how to parry, advance, jump back, lunge, retreat, and hold their saber. Then they paired off with partners and practiced advancing with raised sabers, hitting each other, then retreating. Repeat over and over. Pretty basic stuff.

Wearing my heavy canvas jacket and peering through my wire mesh helmet felt so natural. The checkered wire mesh made things look fuzzy, but I hardly noticed. I liked having my face hidden; the anonymity boosting my courage.

My fingers closed firmly around the sword hilt and a wild energy built up inside me. I longed for real competition. Like when I was in Foils.

I considered challenging Mr. Landreth to a match after class. He was so skillful, I could never win, although I loved to try. Of course if I challenged him, it would be like admitting he was right about fencing being important to me. Too humiliating.

So I said nothing.

As I worked with beginners, a kid named Kevin, who was about my sisters' age, kept asking me for help. I snapped buttons on his jacket, showed him how to hold the saber, found him a new helmet since his was too tight, and offered to be his partner since there were an odd number of students. When his questions got personal (No, I didn't date younger guys and would not give him my number), I quickly matched him with another partner.

Then class was over. We lifted our swords in a goodbye salute.

Reaching up, I removed my helmet and smoothed away loose blond strands.

What a great workout! My skin was damp with sweat and my adrenaline rushed. I was more breathless than I'd expected, and annoyed with myself for being out of shape.

I was thinking about starting a fitness routine, when I sensed someone behind me. Before I could look, I felt a poke of a blunted sword tip in my back. Assuming that Kevin or one of the other beginners was messing around, I turned and found myself face-to-face with a fencer my height, wearing full protective gear.

The unknown fencer lowered his (or her?) saber and said in a muffled voice, "Sabine."

"Huh?" I tried to peer through the wire mesh helmet, but all I could see was black hair and a shadowy face. "Do I know you?"

"I know you."

The masked fencer was slim with an athletic build and definitely not a beginner. I suspected it was a guy, but it was hard to tell through the tinted black mesh.

"Who are you?"

"Want to find out?"

"Sure," I replied, intrigued. I didn't recognize the voice, but something about the fencer's stance was familiar. "How?"

"By fencing."

"Can you handle it?" I retorted. "I used to be a pretty good fencer."

"I still am good. Can you handle it?"

"Definitely."

So I put my helmet back on, bent my knees, and raised my saber. Then I declared in challenge, "En garde."

10

First of all, competitive fencing isn't like what you see in the Zorro movies. Clashing swords, jumping around like an acrobat, and slashing until blood gushes—that's all very dramatic and fun for the movies, but not realistic. Fencing, even with a mysterious stranger who obviously knows who you are but you don't have a clue who he is, is very civilized with rules of right of way.

And quick.

Once a point is scored, fencers stop, retreat, and start over. This all happens in like three seconds. You'd be amazed at how sweaty and exhausting those seconds can be.

I advanced, thrusting out my sword and going for an offensive strike. But my opponent was ready and parried my blow. Metal clashed. I jumped back, feinting retreat, but then advanced again, this time scoring a hit on his helmet. We returned to our marks, and I slapped my sides and said, "Ready. Fence." This time my opponent scored, hitting me on the upper arm.

Around us, I heard excited murmurs. As I readied to start again, I noticed that Mr. Landreth was watching with an amused smile. Was he rooting for my opponent or me? I also realized that my opponent was a guy; slim, wiry, tight arm muscles, and quick graceful movements.

Aware of my teacher watching, I struggled to focus and kept my eyes firmly on my opponent. When the next strike came, I parried. My right arm moved deftly, high for fifth position to block a strike, then lunging forward. Sabers clanged, our pace quickened, and intensity mounted. Sweat dripped down my neck and I breathed heavily. But I didn't drop my gaze, springing forward for another strike and hearing Mr. Landreth call out, "Good one, Sabine!"

But not good enough.

My opponent parried, then struck quick and accurate. If this had been a real battle, I'd have a bloody slash on my arm. He scored the final point and I set my saber down in defeat. Game over.

A new excitement mounted. Now I would find out his identity.

We met in the middle and I watched while he lifted his helmet. First thing I saw was shiny shoulder-length black hair and sparkling ruby stud earrings. His olive skin gleamed with sweat, and his almond-shaped black eyes twinkled.

"Vin!" I exclaimed, totally shocked and delighted. Vin had been one of my favorite people in Foils. He wasn't a macho type like Tony and Derrick, fitting in more with us girls. He was openly gay and had a rowdy sense of humor that made even the most uptight guys comfortable with him.

"Nice form, but too stiff," Vin told me. "Clearly you're out of practice."

"I know," I admitted. "My school didn't have a fencing program."

He looked horrified. "How totally hicksville. You poor girl."

"I didn't mind. I had a lot of great friends there."

"So are you back for good?"

"I'm working on her," Mr. Landreth put in, coming beside us. He rubbed at his goatee and grinned at me. "How about it, Sabine? If you won't take lessons, how about a job?"

"What kind of job?"

"As my assistant. In exchange for private lessons."

"You never offered me a job," Vin griped.

"That's because you have no patience with beginners. A few wanted to quit after your insults."

"Insults are character building. I'm giving them a bonus lesson."

"You're incorrigible," Mr. Landreth murmured. Then he turned back to me. "Seriously, Sabine. You were great with my class. I teach beginners three nights a week and Saturday afternoons. Pick which days work best for you. Do you want the job?"

I felt cornered, yet flattered, too. It would be wonderful to come here regularly and improve my skills. But this was happening too fast.

"I'll have to think about it," I said.

"Think yes," my teacher persisted.

"I'll convince her," Vin said with a wink. He led me over to the benches where he nagged at me to take the job the entire time we put away our equipment. Then he invited me out to lunch at Rosetti's Pizza.

When he said "Rosetti's" I felt a strong shock of déjà vu. Rosetti's not only made the best pizza, it was the place our group always hung out. We'd sit at a back table, debating about fencing techniques, and munching pizza for hours.

I'd always sit by Brianne.

"Come on," Vin urged, not giving me a chance to refuse.

So I went with him. It wasn't until we were entering through the double wood doors of Rosetti's that he told me we wouldn't be alone. And when I saw three familiar faces at the back table, I started to bolt. But Vin anticipated my retreat and parried with a firm grip on my arm as he guided me toward the table.

"I'm going to kill you," I hissed at him. "You knew they'd be here."

"We hang out almost every Saturday."

"You set me up."

"A simple thank you will suffice," he joked.

"You are so dead."

"I love you, too." He laughed and pushed me forward. For a little guy, Vin had a lot of strength. And I was totally drained of energy as I faced Alphonso, Derrick, and his sister Jennae.

My heart thudded and I wasn't sure what to say. When I'd left town, I'd thought I'd never see anyone from Foils again. I hadn't heard from any of them so assumed they felt the same toward me as Brianne, and expected to be as welcome as an outbreak of zits. So I was startled when Jennae squealed my name, then flew over and smothered me in a hug. Her brother Derrick came over, too, smiling widely. Even Alphonso, who was skinny, tall and shy, offered a sincere, "Wel—Welcome back."

"I'm so glad to see you!" Jennae exclaimed. "Sabine. I've missed you!"

"You have?"

"We all have! I can't believe you're really here."

"It's hard for me to believe too."

She stepped back to study me, and I was touched to see tears in her eyes. "You're thinner and different . . . like older. Mature."

"A lot has happened," I admitted with a hesitant smile.

"Well, maturity suits you. You look great."

"Thanks . . . you, too." I wasn't just saying this out of politeness either. Jennae did look fantastic; large-boned and shapely, with creamy skin and long, straight cinnamon hair. She wore multi-strands of beaded jewelry and her own unique style of layered clothes. She was a motherly type and her big smile wrapped around me like a hug.

"So where have you been all this time?" Derrick asked. He was a male version of his sister, only his short hair was darker, he stood a head taller and was thirteen months older. They joked about being Irish twins and mostly got along okay, but when they did argue—watch out.

"I've been living with my grandmother on her farm," I answered.

"In a totally hicksville town without fencing classes," Vin added with a shudder as he sat at the bench table. "I don't know how you stood it."

"I loved the farm with all the animals and woods, and especially being with Nona. The school was cool—I made a lot of friends."

"Anyone special?" Jennae leaned toward me eagerly. "Like a boyfriend?"

"Well . . . yeah." I paused, not comfortable talking about other guys in front of Derrick since we'd gone out a few times. Of course with a close group like Foils, there was lots of inner dating. It was never serious between Derrick and me. He was one of these guys who only talked about cars, which got boring fast.

"What's your guy's name?" Jennae persisted, and for a moment I was reminded of Penny-Love, who always wanted to know romantic buzz. *What was she doing right now?* I wondered. Maybe working in Nona's office and laughing as they discussed new clients? Having a great time without me?

I glanced up to find Jennae, Vin, Alphonso, and Derrick waiting for my answer. I had to think a minute to remember the question.

"His name is Josh," I told them. "He has dark hair and dimples. He's athletic—he likes sports like track and soccer."

"A jock, huh?" Jennae raised her brows. "Does he have a hot body?"

"Very hot." I smiled. "But he isn't all about sports. He's on the student council and volunteers at hospitals to cheer up sick kids."

"Stop already," Vin said, fanning himself. "This guy sounds unreal."

"I never said he was perfect. He has faults, too. He stood me up today."

"The jerk!" Jennae frowned.

"Dump him," Vin added.

Derrick raised his hand jokingly. "I'm still available."

"Been there, not doing it again. Besides Josh didn't mean to ditch me." I quickly explained about Josh's apprenticeship to a professional stage magician and how he couldn't miss out on a great opportunity today. "He'll visit me next weekend."

"Well in that case, he's forgiven," Jennae said. "You must be miserable having to leave him."

"Not just him. I didn't want to leave Sheridan Valley, but Mom insisted. Otherwise I never would, not after—" I stopped myself. Familiar bitterness swelled in my throat and it was hard to talk.

"I understand." Jennae patted my arm soothingly. "And I'm glad you're back."

Then she offered me a slice of pizza.

Who could refuse Rosetti's triple cheese, mushroom, and bacon pizza?

Definitely not me. So I kicked back and enjoyed pizza and conversation. Slipping into old routines felt surreal. Like nothing had changed, yet of course so much had. I wasn't the same person who had stood by defenselessly while being attacked by vicious rumors. I'd gained confidence and new friendships. Looking around, I realized my old friends had changed, too, in subtle ways.

I didn't contribute much to the conversation, preferring to listen and tune into their auras. Jennae radiated like sunshine in her excitement over acing a difficult test and maintaining a 4.0 average so she could apply to a top college. Derrick's orange-brown aura reminded me of autumn as he boasted about skipping college to work as a mechanic in his uncle's body shop. Jennae argued that he still needed college.

"What for?" he retorted. "So I can learn more and earn less?"

Vin's vivid rainbow aura flared as he took Jennae's side. He said only a fool would skip college, then spouted off statistics (which I suspect he made up) about blue-collar jobs versus white-collar jobs.

With a steady green-blue aura, Alphonso remained neutral as always. He never said much because of his stutter. But when he picked up a sword, it was like watching Clark Kent switching into Superman; with chin lifted high, he moved with skillful confidence. I secretly wondered if his stutter was like Clark Kent's glasses; a persona to hide his true self.

Vin, on the other hand, never hid anything. He put it all out there and spoke his mind. After scarfing down the last slice of pizza, he left to order a giant pepperoni. While he was gone, Jennae and Derricks' light banter turned ugly. They argued over who got to use the car tonight. They called each other words I wouldn't repeat. Then they glared and stopped talking completely.

I was trying to think of a way to lighten the mood, when Alphonso tactfully changed the topic. "Hey, Sabine, d—did you hear where Foils is per—performing?"

"No, I haven't. Tell me all about it."

"At a ren—renaissance fair." Alphonso said. "We'll g—go in costumes."

I turned to Jennae. "What's your costume like?"

"Very cool! Tight pants called breeches and shirts with puffy sleeves and ruffles around the neck."

"Fun! And Derrick, are you going in costume, too?"

He nodded, his mouth pursed as if he wasn't ready to give up his fight yet.

But Jennae was warming to the topic. "Vin's cousin has a costume shop and is renting the costumes at a discount," she explained. "We'll act with some faux swords, then switch into our protective gear for performances."

"I'm going to do some jousting," Derrick added.

"I'd love to see that," I said.

"So come watch us," Vin said as he squeezed in beside me. He reached out to place a plastic yellow order number on the edge of the table. "It's in two weeks."

"Please say you'll come," Jennae flashed her dazzling smile at me.

"Yeah," her brother added. "You can applaud for us."

"I can get a costume for you, too," Vin bribed. "You'd look great in Renaissance clothes, especially with such long hair. There's lots of cool stuff to do like watch historical recreations, archery competitions, and lots of great food."

"I can't," I said quickly. "I'll be busy with Josh every weekend."

"Bring him along."

I shook my head firmly. "No."

"Why not?" Vin sounded puzzled.

"It would be too weird. I mean, I'm not in Foils anymore."

"So what? You may have quit the group, but we're all still your friends."

"Not everyone," I pointed out.

"What do you mean?" Jennae sounded hurt.

"You know." I shifted uncomfortably on the beach.

"Actually we don't know." Vin regarded me solemnly. "We felt terrible when people at school were dissing you. Then you were gone and didn't leave a number or address. Your mother wouldn't tell us. Brianne said you dropped her, too."

"I dropped *her*?" I almost fell off the bench.

"Didn't you?" Jennae asked.

"No. She was the one . . ." I paused.

"What?"

"Nothing." I shrugged, not wanting to dredge up that awful time. When I'd seen Brianne's name on the "Kick Sabine Out of School petition," I hadn't read any further, afraid to uncover more back stabbers. Then the next day Mom had my suitcases packed and I moved in with Nona. I was through with everything and everyone connected to Arcadia High.

But now I was finding out Vin, Alphonso, Derrick, and Jennae had never stopped being my friends. Had I been too quick to judge? I had to admit it was good to see them again. Not that it changed anything. I couldn't risk getting sucked back into my old life. After lunch we'd go our separate ways.

A thick pepperoni pizza was delivered to our table and we dug in enthusiastically. I kept telling myself I should leave. Then I'd think, this is our last time together so why not hang out a little longer? I loved talking about fencing. It was exhilarating to discuss stuff like the most effective competition blade, favorite helmet styles, and the unfairness of biased referees.

We were talking about the National Competition when gazes shifted beyond me. The table went silent like a vacuum had sucked out all the air. I heard a choked cry from behind me. Swiveling in my seat, I saw a slim girl with gold highlights woven in short brown hair. Her face was ashen, her gray eyes wide, and her mouth gaping open in shock as she stared at me.

Brianne.

11

Brianne's expression was so horrified that I found myself glancing around to make sure Kip's head wasn't floating nearby. But no sign of a ghost, although the energy at our table seemed supernatural.

"Ohmygod!" Brianne cried. "Sabine!"

I just sat there, stunned.

"What are you doing here?" she demanded.

"Leaving." I pushed my chair back.

"No, you stay. I'm going."

"Don't bother. I should never have come here."

She didn't reply, but the fury in her eyes slashed to my heart. There was no mistake about her feelings. She hated me.

"Vin, take me home," I said firmly, steeling my emotions so I wouldn't break. I couldn't let Brianne know how deeply she hurt me, how close I was to tears. What had I ever done to her? Except be her friend.

"But Sabine, I haven't finished my pizza," Vin complained, wiping off a string of cheese from his chin.

"We can't part Vin from his pizza," Jennae said with a flash of her big smile. She reached out for Brianne's arm. "Come on, Bree. Let's just sit down and enjoy this delicious pizza."

"I lost my appetite," Brianne said.

"Sit here," Derrick offered, pointing to the spot farthest from me.

She shook her head. "I'm leaving."

"Me, too," I added.

I tried to go, but Vin kept a firm grip on my arm. He looked between us and spoke calmly, "Girls, what's going on?"

"Nothing!" we both replied. Brianne and I looked at everyone, embarrassed, then quickly turned away.

"Ooh . . . intense hostility," Vin said. "Clearly you two have issues to work out."

"Not me!" Brianne snapped. "I don't know what you're talking about."

"So you have no problems with Sabine?"

"Of course not."

Vin eyed her sternly. "Then there's no reason for you to rush off. Is there, Brianne?"

"Well I . . . I guess not."

"And Sabine?" he asked me pointedly.

I lifted my head with forced casualness. "No problems here."

"Oh, all right." Brianne tossed back her silky hair. "But there better be plenty of pizza, because I'm starving."

"Dig in." Derrick gestured to the table, smiling as if he didn't notice how Brianne made a big circle of the table to avoid me, taking a seat far at the opposite end. "We'll have enough pizza for the others, too, when they show up. You heard from them, Bree?"

"Only Tony and Annika. They'll be here soon."

"Annika?" I asked before I could stop myself. "Who's she?"

Brianne ignored me and poured a glass of water. But Vin was quick to answer. "Annika joined Foils several months ago—she replaced Tiffany."

I wanted to ask who replaced me. Instead I asked, "What happened to Tiffany?"

"She moved to Idaho. We also had two brothers join, Izziah and Mark Wyllie. If there's an opening, you could join again."

I shook my head firmly. "I already told you I'm not returning to Arcadia."

Brianne smirked, and I could tell this was good news to her. And again I wondered what I had done to cause her betrayal? We'd been so close. We shared everything and I trusted her with my deepest secrets. I know she trusted me, too.

While conversation shifted to people I didn't know, I focused in on Brianne. She was thinner and wore more makeup than I remembered. She spoke in an unnaturally cheerful voice, averting her gaze from me. When she reached for pizza, I noticed a tattoo on her arm. It was a faery. Hurt pierced so deep, I had to look away.

Had it only been last spring we'd had the tattoo conversation?

"My simple philosophy about life is easy," Brianne had declared during our ritual weekend sleepover. It was warm outside so we were bunking in sleeping bags in my treehouse. We had snacks, a CD player, and flashlights. We were so tired we were just rambling on about life, love, and other philosophical stuff.

"What's easy about life?" I murmured sleepily, glancing over to where she lie on her back, her flashlight making a yellow moon on the wood ceiling.

"Life isn't easy, that's what I'm saying. So you have to find the fun in everything and not sweat the small stuff. Just wear gray sweatpants every day, a comfortable T-shirt, and get a tattoo. That's all there is to it."

"A tattoo? What design?"

"A faery."

"Cool. I'll get one, too."

"We'll do it together. Friendship and being happy are like the most important things. We're only going to be around for what? Seventy, eighty years? So enjoy life now. I'm gonna enjoy mine in comfy clothes and a tattoo."

After that she went around wearing sweats and corny tie-dyed shirts, but she promised to wait for the tattoo so we could get them together.

"Hey, Sabine!" I looked up to find Vin snapping his fingers at me.

"Huh?" I blinked.

"I asked what's been going on with you? Other than the hot boyfriend," Vin added with a wink.

"Not much, just school and stuff." Stuff involving deadly predictions, ghosts, and spirit guides. Of course I didn't say that.

"So what about a new school?"

"Don't know. Probably a private school. My mother has something planned." And I was *not* eager to find out. Mom's attempt to talk with me this morning increased my unease. *Please don't let her make me return to Arcadia,* I thought. *Anywhere else!*

Vin went on about different schools in the area, but my gaze wandered over to Brianne. She was obvious in her avoidance of me, yet no one else seemed to notice. I had a wild urge to scream out "Betrayer!" Then I'd demand to know why she'd turned against me. I mean, we'd been closer than sisters, and I'd trusted her completely. What had gone wrong?

I'd replayed our last conversation in my mind so many times, searching for a hint of trouble ahead and finding none. We'd been hanging out in her room listening to music like usual. She was in an unusually good mood, excited to tell me her big news. Tony, who was a year older, had invited her to the prom.

"Of course I said yes!" she squealed."I thought I'd have to wait till I was a junior to go to a prom."

"But Tony?" I questioned. "You told me he was an opinionated, chauvinistic jerk? You don't like him that way."

"Did I say I was in love with him? No. I'm just going to have fun at a dance."

"The prom," I said pointedly. "That's kind of serious."

"He knows it isn't serious. It's just for kicks, you know, like when you went out with Derrick."

"We only went to a movie—not even a very good one—and when he kissed me his breath tasted like garlic."

"Not into vampires?" she joked.

"Definitely not into Derrick. And it was mutual."

"My point exactly. I'm not interested in Tony either. But I already have this gorgeous strapless red dress picked out. After we have a great time at the prom, I'll tell him I just want to be friends. Besides, I've got my eye on one of his friends."

I could tell her mind was made up already, so I dropped the subject. Then we practiced dance moves in front of her mirror, laughing at ourselves. I had no idea this would be the last time we'd laugh together.

Now my lips tightened into a deep frown as I watched Brianne ignore me. Enough already. I didn't need this kind of abuse.

I was going to announce I had to leave when I heard a boisterous voice boom, "Now the party can start—we're here!"

Turning, I saw Tony walking toward the table with a pretty dark-skinned girl with light eyes and spiked brown hair. She was a foot shorter than

Tony who was over six feet. They made a cute, if height-challenged, couple.

"Tony and Annika! You made it!" Vin said a bit too heartily. "What was keeping you?"

"Practice, man. And it was hell," Tony added with a grimace. "Only one more game of the season and we gotta win."

"You will," Annika said in a little girl voice that was softer than a whisper. The gaze she gave Tony glowed with admiration.

"Man, I'm starving. Pizza looks good."

I shifted on the bench so Tony and Annika could sit together. But Tony ignored Annika and walked around the table. He slipped in the seat next to Brianne and wrapped a muscular arm around her shoulders. "Hey, babe. Been waiting long?"

"Too long without you." Brianne sort of melted against Tony and murmured, "Missed you."

Then she lifted her chin to kiss Tony.

I nearly barfed.

12

When I whispered to Vin that I wanted to leave now, he pretended not to hear and gestured to me like I was a grand prize being revealed on a game show. "Tony, check it out," he said with a wave of his arm. "Look who's here."

"No, shit! Sabine!" Tony's hazel eyes widened as he grinned. "What the hell brings you back?"

"Me." Vin proudly pointed to himself. "I brought her."

"Against my will," I said like it was a joke.

"I found her at Landreth's class."

"You're taking classes with Landreth?" Tony asked.

I said "no" at the same time Vin said "yes."

Tony seemed to think this was comical and slapped Vin on the shoulder. "Man, get your stories straight. I'd rather hear from Sabine anyway." He turned to me. "You back for good?"

I shrugged, surprised by Tony's warm welcome. We'd never been close, although we got along fine at Foils. He had a dynamic personality that made him the life of every party. But I'd never been much for partying.

He was still grinning at me. "It's cool to see you."

"It is?" I didn't quite believe him.

"Sure." His arm tightened around Brianne, possessively. "You were one hell of a fencer and tight with my girl. You and Bree gotta have lots to catch up on."

"There's no rush," Brianne said curtly.

"Another time," I added.

"If Sabine has to leave, we can't stop her."

"And you're the expert on getting me to leave," I snapped.

Brianne turned completely pale. I immediately felt guilty for lashing out at her. A part of me wanted to apologize and talk things out. But I reminded myself we weren't friends anymore. She'd forfeited that role when she signed the petition.

So I took Vin firmly by the arm. "We're leaving. Now."

A string of cheese dangled from his mouth and he wiped it off, frowning at me. "But I haven't finished my pizza."

"You've had enough," I said unsympathetically. "And so have I."

Then with a curt goodbye, I left Rosetti's. I could feel the intensity of gazes following me out of the room; curious and hostile.

On the drive back to the Center (where I left the car Mom had loaned me), I hardly said a word. Vin did his best to get me to talk, but I was sick inside, like I'd eaten something toxic. And I couldn't forget the cold way Brianne had looked at me. That hurt more than I wanted to admit even to myself.

When the car was stopped at a red light, Vin reached out to squeeze my hand. "Are you okay, Sabine?"

"Yeah."

"What's with you and Brianne? I guessed you'd had an argument since she wouldn't talk about you after you left. But it's more than an argument, isn't it?"

I shrugged. "I don't really know."

"The same way you didn't know Kip Hurst was going to die?"

"This has nothing to do with Kip," I snapped.

"Fine, don't talk about it. Be rude to the guy who's been your chauffeur and bought you the best pizza in the world. I'm of no importance."

"I never said that—"

"Whatever." The light changed and he stomped hard on the gas.

My head started to throb, and I turned toward the window. It had been a total mistake to come with Vin. What was I thinking? That I just could return like nothing had happened? I must have been momentarily insane.

There was no going back—especially with Brianne.

When Vin dropped me off at my car, I thanked him for the ride. We spoke politely and I told him I'd see him around. Only I didn't mean it.

I'd had my first and last reunion with Foils.

Once in the privacy of my (well, Mom's) car, I turned on the engine and switched to a hard rock station, volume blasting. Shutting out thoughts, feelings, and memories, I got lost in the song.

An empty house greeted me. No one was at home. Mom must still be out with my sisters, and I assumed Dad was at his office. In silence, my own thoughts seemed to shout.

I had all this nervous energy and wasn't sure how to channel it. So I went to my room and tried to channel Opal for advice. I closed my eyes and whispered Opal's name. I waited and waited. Nothing. I even tried to summon Kip's ghost. But another dead end (no pun intended).

Checking my email, there was the usual spam and one surprising message—from Thorn! I hadn't heard from her since she'd found out I was leaving town and accused me of being a wimp for not standing up to my mother and refusing to move back. She was right, of course, but I couldn't admit that. So we just stopped talking, and I'd felt bad, worrying that she was angry with me. Eagerly, I clicked the email open.

She didn't apologize (not her style) but just talked like usual. She was busy, helping out this guy named K.C. who was homeless. She was showing him how to fill out papers for financial assistance and appoint a new guardian. Thorn said she'd visit when things settled down.

She closed her message with, "Miss you, Beth." Which I knew was her way of apologizing because none of her other friends knew her real name. I'd only found out by accident and gained her trust by keeping it a secret.

I skimmed through the other emails, then I turned on the TV and laid down on my bed. I switched channels until I settled on MTV.

My eyes felt heavy and next thing I knew I was dreaming . . .

I was in a car, going way too fast. When I looked closely at the driver, I jumped with shock—Kip.

He wore a formal suit, but his tie had been tossed aside on the empty passenger seat, tangled around crushed rose petals. There was a furious energy in the car, emanating from Kip. He strangled the steering wheel in a death grip. He was beyond anger, pushing the car to go faster. Under his breath, he was swearing as the speedometer rose from eighty to ninety and kept climbing higher.

"Slow down," I tried to tell him.

He focused ahead, ripping the wheel to the right to avoid another car.

"Kip, please slow down!" I tried again.

But he didn't hear me, as I was nothing more than air. He waved his fist toward the windshield and shouted, "Got to get her!"

Was he chasing someone? I tried to see through the windows. There was only a blur of lights from buildings and a few cars whizzing by.

The speedometer jumped past 100 and even without a solid body I could smell the strong odor of alcohol. How much had he been drinking? He was acting crazy. Where was he going in such a hurry? I could see the glowing clock on his dash and it was almost two in the morning.

Looking at his formal suit and crushed flowers, I realized what night this was. Then it all made horrible sense. Prom night—Kip's last night on earth. He must have already dropped off his date Aileen.

But what had caused his murderous rage?

We were climbing, going away from the city and into the darkened hills. But he continued on, his fury building with each mile. The car swayed wildly around corners, nearly tipping over. He didn't hear my screams or know my terror, as if our roles had reversed and I was the ghost.

"Damn you!" he shouted suddenly, and for a second I thought he meant me. Only he didn't even know I was there.

His aura was dark and terrifying. I wanted to escape, but I was trapped beside him. Again, I tried to talk to him, begging him to stop; as if I could somehow change past events.

A truck honked a horn, swerving out of Kip's way. But Kip only accelerated, bent over the wheel, whipped into a critical frenzy.

The car was swerving more wildly, but Kip didn't seem aware. His face reflected pale death. I wanted to grab him, force him stop, but this moment was racing out of control, with only one outcome possible.

We turned a corner, and the tree loomed ahead. Darker than night with twisted branches that beckoned like crooked fingers.

Closer, closer, closer.

Then we crashed.

13

When I awoke, soft dawn light cast wispy shadows around my room. Disoriented, for an uneasy moment I expected to see the twisted tree and a car wreck. Instead, my room was quiet. I remembered leaving the TV on, yet it was silent and the remote control lay on the bedside dresser. My clothes had been picked up from the carpet where I'd left them.

Who'd been in here? Mom? She hadn't cleaned up after me since I was a little girl.

Glancing at the clock, I saw it was almost seven. Despite my disturbing dream, I'd slept through the night.

It wasn't an ordinary dream, Opal spoke in my head.

"Then what was it?" I asked without speaking, closing my eyes to get a clearer vision of my spirit guide. She wore a jeweled turban and her dark brows knitted together solemnly.

A memory transference.

"It felt more real than a memory, I was there in the car with Kip."

Your astral self journeyed through the past. You invited the experience upon yourself by calling forth Kip's spirit. He didn't have the energy to come to you directly, so he sent you to his memories. An intriguing learning opportunity that should offer new insights.

"Intriguing? It was terrifying! I was trapped in that car and it kept going faster and faster until we crashed. It was worse than a nightmare."

It was only an illusion and you were perfectly safe.

"I didn't feel safe," I grumbled, gathering my blankets around my shoulders. "And I still don't know who Kip wants me to help or why he was driving so fast. Can't you just bend rules and tell me?"

I am bound by no rules, as you naively assume. Nor am not privy to higher knowledge. Your journey through another's mind was a gift from this side; a glimpse into the past. I would expect you to show gratitude rather than offer complaints.

"I'm not complaining," I argued.

Sounds like complaining to me.

"I'm just confused."

As fear is a gift of energy to aid in focusing your talents, confusion inspires curiosity; opening windows of creativity and inviting resourceful insights. Embrace your confusion and seek out inventive solutions. Answers will follow.

"While I'm doing this embracing, what are you going to do to help?"

I'm always a thought away, watching over you.

"Then why don't you always answer me?"

When you don't hear my reply, the answer is no.

"You're not helping."

My role is to guide so that you may find your inner light. Her regal head lifted with amusement. *Besides, I have a full life here, with numerous engagements. I'd tell you all about it, but I must be off. My dear friend Lucretia awaits . . .*

Then she was gone.

I sat up in bed and kicked aside my covers. A lot of help Opal was. While she was off with Lucretia, I was left with a pile of problems. And I still didn't know who Kip wanted me to help.

My initial guess, Leanna, didn't seem likely after viewing Kip's memory. Something had happened at the prom or afterwards. Kip had been furious and rushing after someone. "Got to get her," he'd said.

Was this the same "her" he wanted me to help?

The most logical girl was his date Aileen. According to news reports, Aileen and Kip had a great time at the prom and everything was fine when he dropped her off. But in my dream Kip had been far from fine—he'd been furious. Had he and Aileen gotten into an argument? Maybe Aileen cheated on him with another guy and Kip found out. Wild with jealously, Kip drove away, and lost control of his car.

When Aileen found out about the crash, she must have felt horribly guilty. No wonder she didn't tell anyone what happened.

Was that why Kip's ghost appeared to me? To help Aileen get over her grieving? Kip must still love her a lot and wanted to send her a message that he was all right. So he'd turned to the only person he knew with a connection to the other side.

Damn him anyway!

Well, he came to the wrong person. I'd tried to help him once and ended up being blamed for his death. If I showed up at his girlfriend's house, she'd probably call the police. When people heard I was back in town, old rumors would buzz again.

Even if I enrolled in a secluded private school, I wouldn't be able to escape notice for long. Eventually someone would connect me with Kip's death. Then one person would tell another and another until my reputation was totally trashed. I wouldn't be able to go anywhere without people pointing at me.

Passing on messages from the dearly departed was not the way to keep a low profile. And I definitely couldn't help someone who didn't want my help. I didn't even know Aileen; she was older and

Arcadia High was a large school. I had a vague idea who she was from a picture in a newspaper. But I couldn't even remember her last name, something beginning with a "P" or maybe a "B." I think her family owned some kind of restaurant.

If Aileen was suffering from guilt issues, she needed a shrink not a psychic. Her mental health was not my problem. I had more than enough problems of my own, like missing Nona and my friends, plus starting over at a new school.

Ironically, Mom thought she was doing me a favor by insisting I move back to San Jose. How could I tell her my true feelings without coming off like a selfish brat? Mom and I were so different, we got along better living apart. If I told her I'd rather live with Nona, she'd take it personally and our relationship would be worse than ever.

So I said nothing.

Shifting uncomfortably in my bed, I realized I hadn't spoken to Nona since leaving. I'd expected her to call, but she hadn't. Was it because she was too busy? Or had her illness worsened? I should be there, watching over her. If I didn't hear from Nona by this afternoon, I'd call her myself.

Glancing around my tastefully decorated bed-room, I longed to be back at Nona's home in my cozy attic room. Instead of looking out on traffic and a sea of suburbia, I'd view a panorama of green treetops, blue skies, and wild birds.

A large reddish brown bird fluttered at my window, as if my thoughts were magic. I chuckled at the coincidence. Then I gasped. I knew that bird!

"Dagger!" I jumped off my bed and rushed to the window.

The falcon flapped his wings and regarded me with golden dark eyes.

"Come inside," I invited, opening the latch.

But he squawked in a clear refusal. With a powerful swish of his wings, he tucked his head and dive-bombed to the ground. That's when I looked down and saw someone waving up at me.

Dominic.

My heart did some fluttering of its own, and I glanced down with embarrassment at the wrinkled shirt I was wearing and my tangled blond hair. After restless dreams, I'm sure I could use some makeup, too.

Dominic grinned up at me. I put my finger to my lips, gesturing so he'd know the rest of the family was asleep. What was he doing here so early? Not that I cared about the reason; I was ridiculously happy to see him. After brushing my hair, putting on some makeup, and getting dressed, I hurried outside.

Dominic looked even better up close, and it took all my self-control not to throw my arms around him. I told myself I was just relieved to see someone from Sheridan Valley. I would have been just as excited if Penny-Love or Thorn showed up. But who was I kidding?

I couldn't wipe the goofy smile from my face, and frankly I didn't even try.

"What are you doing here?" I asked him, holding my hands together so I wouldn't do anything dumb like touch him.

"Talking to you," he said. Dagger circled overhead and settled on a tall branch as if he was getting a good seat to watch the Dominic and Sabine show.

"I doubt you drove two hours just to talk with me." In my mind I saw a flash of silver jewelry. "The missing charm! That's what this is about. Are you tracking down a new lead?"

He gave me a long look before answering. "Yeah."

"That's great! I wondered why you were here so early." I smiled although I felt a little disappointed that he was only here because of the charms. Not that I expected him to drive so far just to see me. That would be crazy. Right?

"Sorry if I woke you," he told me.

"You didn't."

"I would have waited for you to wake."

"Well . . . thanks." I glanced down at the dewy lawn. "So tell me more. What have you found out?"

"The woman with the last charm lives in Pacific Grove."

"Isn't that near Monterey?"

"Yeah. I'm headed there."

"Are you inviting me to go with you?"

He grin offered a challenge. "Are you accepting?"

"As if you could leave me behind. Of course I'm going."

"Sure you don't have any other plans?"

"Nothing I want to do," I admitted, thinking of Kip's girlfriend and his request to her help.

"Is there something you *don't* want to do?" he asked curiously.

"Only if I want all the vicious rumors about me to start up again and risk getting chased out of town." I was joking but something clicked in my head. Getting chased out of town? Not a bad idea.

Mom had asked me back as a reward for behaving normally. Because I was doing well in school and had a respectable boyfriend, she assumed I'd outgrown my "childish" interest in the other side. But what if she found out I still talked to ghosts and old rumors started spreading again?

Easy answer: Mom would ship me straight back to Nona's.

Which was exactly where I wanted to be.

14

If helping a ghost would help me return to Nona's, I was ready to get started. That meant visiting Kip's girlfriend. When I mentioned this to Dominic, he offered to drive me. That was one of the cool things about Dominic; how he was always willing to help out without any prying questions. He waited on the porch while I rushed back inside to look for Aileen's address. Although I didn't know her personally, I had an idea how to find her.

It didn't take long to search through a desk drawer crammed with old school papers, letters, and cards for a wrinkled newspaper clipping. Last May, when I'd cut it from the newspaper, I'd had a sudden insight that I would be leaving home soon. So I'd buried the clipping in a drawer, then pulled out my suitcases. That evening my mother told me she was sending me to live with my grandmother. Mom had expected me to argue or at least act surprised, but she'd been the one who'd gasped when she saw my packed suitcases.

Starting over at Nona's had turned out to be the best thing ever. And now, unfolding the clipping, I longed desperately to return to Sheridan Valley. Nona needed me and I needed to be with her. I would do *anything* to make that happen.

The headline read: *Tragedy Strikes Local Sports Star*. Steeling my emotions, I scanned until I found the name of Kip's prom date.

"Aileen Palendini," I murmured triumphantly. "I knew her last name started with either B or P. And her family owns Chopsticks Cafe."

Doing a quick online search for the restaurant, I found out its hours, location, and even a complete menu. Unfortunately, there was no personal information on the Palendini family. But the restaurant opened at noon, so I could go there later.

As I left my room, it occurred to me that I shouldn't leave without telling someone. Not that my parents would notice I was gone. The longest conversation I'd had with Dad since moving back consisted of him asking if I had a nice day before he disappeared into his office. And Mom's committees and appointments kept her busy. Still if Mom found my bedroom empty, she might overreact and put out an Amber Alert like I was a missing kid.

So I propped a note where Mom was sure to see it, by the coffee maker:

Out with a friend. Back soon.
~Sabine

Then I hurried outside to join Dominic.

That's when I got a look at his new truck. Shining new sticker-still-in-the window latest model truck. A duo-wheeled, burgundy four-door Dodge quarter-ton pickup with long bed and chrome hub caps. A huge improvement over his previous wheels.

"Wow!" I murmured.

"Not bad, huh?" He casually leaned against the truck bed, a proud grin lighting up his usually serious face.

I wanted to ask how he could afford a new truck on a handyman's salary, but I had a feeling he wouldn't tell me. For all I know he could have won the lottery or was secretly the heir to a wealthy empire. More likely, he'd bought it on credit.

Dominic spouted off the size of the engine, the mileage, and other auto facts as I climbed inside. I patted the leather seats appreciatively, inhaling the tangy new car smell. Through the open window, I heard a screech overhead and glanced up to see Dagger circling high in his air expressway.

Dominic caught my glance. "Dagger isn't used to my truck yet."

"If I had wings, I'd fly, too," I said as I slipped on my seat belt. "No congested Bay Area traffic. Total freedom."

"Flying works for birds, but I'd rather drive this baby."

"Typical guy."

He laughed. We both knew he was far from typical.

"Admit it," he said, leaning toward me with a grin. "You love my truck, too."

"I wouldn't call it love, more of a friendship."

"Only friendship?" he asked, raising one dark brow.

"Well . . ." Something in his gaze unnerved me and brought back the memory of his face close to mine and a deep kiss. Not somewhere I wanted to go. "Hey, the truck is hot, but I wouldn't want Josh to get jealous."

"Doubtful."

"What do you mean by that?" I demanded.

"You don't want to hear it."

"You can't possibly find fault with him. All he does is help other people, like volunteering at hospitals and working on committees at school."

"He's a real saint," Dominic said in a tone that meant something different.

Definitely treading dangerous waters here, so I abruptly changed course. "How's Nona doing?" I asked.

"Fine." He'd turned away from me, focusing on the road.

"I've been worried she might be working too hard."

"She thrives on hard work. You know your grandmother."

"Yes, I do. That's why I worry." I hesitated, then added, "If everything's okay, why hasn't she called me?"

"Have you tried calling her?"

"Well . . . no." I shook my head. "I was waiting for her to call first."

"Maybe she's waiting, too—giving you time with your family."

"She's family, too. Besides, in an over-achieving family like mine, I have too much time. Usually alone, while they're off doing their thing." I didn't want to sound pathetic, so I added, "Not that I've been bored. Yesterday I helped out my former fencing instructor with some new students."

"Cool. I'd like to learn fencing." He took a left turn, one hand lightly turning the wheel and the other resting inches from my seat.

"It takes a lot of practice and is harder than it looks."

"So teach me."

"Me?" I imagined putting my hand over his to demonstrate how to grip a sword. Touching arms, pressing against his firm body . . . definitely *not* a good idea.

So I told him I didn't give lessons, then I switched the topic to our search for Nona's missing remedy book. The three charms we had were supposed to be clues to the book's location. But it was hard to figure out a century-old meaning to a silver cat, fish, and house.

"I figure the book's in Nevada because of the quality of silver used to mold the charms," Dominic said. "They could represent a town. Something like Cat Creek or Troutdale."

"Are those real places?"

He shrugged, slowing for a yield sign. "I can find out."

"Could the charms mean a name? Maybe there was a woman named Kitty Fishhouse."

"Or a business . . . ever heard of cat houses?"

I blushed and smacked him lightly on the arm. Then I sank into my seat with a sigh. "It's seems so impossible. After all this time, Kitty would be dust and any house would be long gone."

"We'll find the last charm," Dominic insisted. "Soon."

"We have to." I tried not to think what would happen if Nona's illness worsened before we found the remedy book. Her memory was already failing. How long before she no longer recognized me and lapsed into a coma?

When we turned off on highway 101, I asked Dominic if I should check a map.

He shook his head. "Not necessary."

"You already have directions?"

"Don't need them."

I glanced at him, not just seeing Dominic but also a flash of him as a young child, with blond hair and scabbed knees, chasing through thick shrubbery after a large gray dog. "You lived around here once?"

"Stay out of my head," he said, sounding more amused than angry.

"So I'm right?"

"You know you are."

"But I don't know much about you. When did you live around here?"

"Before Mom got sick, we lived in San Juan Baptista."

"On Olympia Road," I said without thinking.

"You're doing it again," he accused.

"Sorry." But I really wasn't because I was really curious about Dominic's past.

He rarely talked about his childhood and I knew he was hiding disturbing secrets. Once I'd connected with him so deeply, I'd had a terrible vision of when he'd been a child and an abusive uncle chained him outside like a wild animal. While this gave him an uncanny connection to animals, it distanced him from people. It was like he put up a mental fence with posted warnings to "Keep Out."

Yet sometimes I glimpsed his thoughts, which was really strange because I couldn't read minds. Visions, yes. Prophetic dreams, yes. But mind-reading? No. Except occasional flashes when I had a strong connection with people, like my sisters and Nona. So why did I get these insights with Dominic, too? Maybe because we were both intuitive.

A short while later we pulled into a trailer park off First Street, several miles from the ocean. Dominic checked a piece of paper. "Bettina Sinclair. Yellow trailer with gnomes in the garden."

As we stepped out of the truck, I looked for Dagger, but saw only sea gulls overhead.

Bettina Sinclair, a fiftyish woman with wispy dark hair, reminded me of one of the gnomes in her garden. Short, squat with rosy cheeks, and furry slippers peaked from underneath her billowing flowered blue muumuu. She even wore dangly mushroom earrings.

"Good morning," Dominic greeted politely. "Are you Mrs. Sinclair?"

She nodded. "You must be Dominic."

"Yes. And this is Sabine Rose—the girl I told you about who may be a distant relative of yours."

As Mrs. Sinclair looked at me, her expression changed to astonishment. "Your hair! The stories are true!"

I touched my hair self-consciously. "What stories?" I asked.

"The ones my grandfather told me about his great-grandmother having the mark of a seer, a dark streak in pale blond hair. Like yours," she added, fanning her face and breathing fast. "When I was little, my sister and I would play 'seer' by putting powder in our hair except for one dark streak. I always yearned for lovely blond hair like yours. Of course this proves we are indeed related."

I wasn't sure how to respond. I just nodded.

"But I'm afraid you've both traveled a long way for nothing," the short woman went on. "I wanted to call back, but didn't have a number."

"What do you mean?" Dominic asked. "You told me on the phone that you had the silver charm in an old trunk."

"Yes. I inherited Grandfather's belongings, including all jewelry. I vaguely remember an old necklace with some kind of dangling charm."

"What was it shaped like?" I asked eagerly.

"Who remembers?" She waved her hand. "But it was old and tarnished and I remember thinking silver cleaner would shine it up real pretty. Only I never got around to it, and now the trunk is gone." Mrs. Sinclair gave an apologetic flutter of her hand. "I have a stinking suspicion who took it, too."

I exchanged a startled glance with Dominic.

"I should have known she'd pull something like this," she added with an angry stomp on the doorstep. "That conniving, greedy, lying bitch. And to think I trusted her!"

"A friend of yours?" I guessed.

"Worse." Mrs. Sinclair scowled. "My sister."

15

As I climbed back into Dominic's truck, I tasted salty air and disappointment.

Mrs. Sinclair explained that her older sister Izzabelle felt she'd been cheated out of her inheritance, and that the trunk belonged to her since she was the eldest. "We don't talk much, and I wondered why she showed up last month. Now I know," Mrs. Sinclair said bitterly. Then she told us she was through with her sister. She sounded so hurt, reminding me how I felt when I'd found out about Brianne.

"Another dead end," I said as we drove away.

"Not an end. A delay." Dominic offered me an encouraging smile, flipping the turn sign to merge onto highway 101. "We have Izzabelle's address, so we'll find the charm. Now I'm going to take you to see your friend."

"My friend?" I blinked. "Oh, you must mean Aileen."

"Don't you want to see her?"

"Sure. But it's complicated," I added doubtfully. "We aren't exactly friends."

This only spurred his curiosity. Since we had plenty of time to talk and he understood my connection to the other side, I explained about Kip. It felt good to share my story with someone who wouldn't roll his eyes like I was crazy.

"That's cool you're helping a ghost," he said when I finished.

"Most people would think it was weird, not cool."

"Am I most people?"

He gave me a deep look that made my cheeks warm. I ignored the jump of my heart and gave a casual shrug. "Anyway, Aileen probably won't talk to me."

"Then let me talk to her first."

"And say what? 'Excuse me, but I have a message from your dead boyfriend.'"

"A definite attention grabber." Dominic chuckled, and I found myself thinking that Dominic already had *my* attention. I liked being with him, talking to him, looking at him. I noticed how lines deepened around his blue eyes when he smiled. There was a tiny rip in the right leg of his jeans, maybe from barbed wire from the pasture fencing. And those jeans fit snug.

He kept one hand on the steering wheel, his gaze shifting to the rearview mirror then over to me, and sometimes lingering on me. I wondered what he was thinking, if he was remembering that moment after the truck accident when he held me and whispered, "I love you." We hadn't talked about any of this, I mean, it wasn't right. Not fair to Josh.

A short while later we parked at Chopsticks. The parking lot was packed; a good indication of great food. My stomach rumbled, reminding me I'd skipped lunch.

But food would have to wait.

Dominic waved at me, then disappeared inside the small restaurant. I leaned out the truck window, inhaling delicious food smells. Overhead I heard a squawk and saw that Dagger was back. It was odd how the wild bird stayed so close to Dominic. I respected Dominic's connection to wild creatures, although I didn't understand it. When I asked about it, he always gave vague answers.

He was so damned secretive. I could make a list of the things I knew about him and not go into double digits. I didn't even know his full name!

Dominic . . . what? Smith, Miller, or Johnson? Dominic Smith . . . Nah, that didn't sound right. Something as ordinary as a last name shouldn't be a big secret. Hmmm . . . there must be a way to find out.

His brand new truck! Dominic must have filled out a registration and other paperwork. There was nothing on the dashboard, so I popped open the glove box. There was a large owner's manual on the truck, napkins, sunglasses, a packet of almonds, and assorted official papers. Just as I reached for these papers, I heard my name being called and saw Dominic returning.

Quickly, I shoved the papers back and slammed the glove box. Then I sat up in my seat, smiling innocently like nothing had happened.

"Hey," I greeted him casually. "How'd it go?"

"Better than expected." He yanked open my door. "Come on, Sabine."

I raised my brows. "Where?"

"Inside. Aileen wants to talk with you."

"Are you sure? She doesn't even know me."

"She knows who you are. Even got excited when I said you were here. Wants to talk to you. Privately."

"But why?" I didn't quite believe what I was hearing.

"Go find out. I'll wait here."

I bit my lip, struck by a strong urge to climb back in the truck and get out of here. But then I'd never find any answers. And I had a feeling I was close to learning something important.

What could Aileen want from me? I wondered as I reached for the door of the restaurant. We'd never met and I only had a fuzzy idea of what she looked like.

Our only connection was a dead guy.

* * *

Aileen's black ponytails were held into place with wooden chopsticks. She was petite and moved in a quick, bouncy way that reminded me of a bunny— a very nervous bunny. I noticed her anxiously biting her lip as she waved me to a private corner of the restaurant. We sat across from each other at a small rounded table with a gold-fringed tablecloth.

"You wanted to talk to, uh, me?" I asked cautiously, clasping my hands on the table. "About Kip?"

"Yeah . . . about my Kip." Her aura, gray with despair, was like a heavy blanket smothering me.

"I didn't really know him," I told her. *At least not while he was alive.*

"But you knew he was going to die."

"I wasn't sure—it was just a dream."

"A dream that happened," she said sadly.

I nodded grimly. This whole conversation felt surreal. I'd expected Kip's girlfriend to hate me, but she seemed happy to see me.

"You were the messenger, that's all," she said sadly. "I've read up on psychics and supernatural experiences since . . . well, you know."

I nodded, at a loss for words. Her waves of grief rolled over me, her aura had no colors, only a dreary gray fog.

"At least you tried to help, which was more than anyone else did . . . including me." Abruptly, she stood and reached for a silver pitcher. "Would you like some water?"

"No, thanks." She poured herself a glass and I had a feeling she was stalling, deciding what to tell me. But why tell me anything? Why even talk to me?

"Are you all right?" I asked gently.

"I haven't been all right for over six months. Can you believe he's been gone that long already? I still think of him every day. He was more than my boyfriend, we were soul mates, and I thought we were going to be together—" Her voice broke. "Together forever."

"I'm so sorry."

She looked away, taking a sip of water. "I've wanted to talk to you since . . . after."

"Why?" I asked softly.

"Because you got a raw deal. Only I didn't know for a while. At first I was in bad shape and seriously depressed," she confessed. "My parents thought I might do something dumb—which I wouldn't—and made me see a doctor and take pills. I was so messed up, I cried for weeks. When I was recovered enough to return to school, I heard you'd been forced to leave."

"Not exactly forced. I moved in with my grandmother."

"But it was totally unfair. I felt awful when I found out. Arcadia High is full of morons."

"No argument there," I said with a wry smile.

"Kip would have been furious if he knew."

"Oh, he knows," I murmured. He wasn't furious, though, and seemed more intent on his own issues. Death hadn't improved him *that* much.

She leaned closer, scrutinizing me. "Can you tell me . . . how is he? I know you're special, that you know things."

"I don't know that much, except he cares about you a lot."

"I miss him so much," she said, her eyes shining, "Everyone knew we'd hooked up, but no one knew how it was so, you know, serious. You've seen him, right? So he must have told you that we were engaged."

"Engaged!" My hand jerked, hitting the table and shaking her water glass. "But you're too young."

"Who says? Age doesn't matter, besides my parents were crazy about him and were excited about our engagement. He didn't get a chance to tell his family. We planned to get married after graduation, and he was saving up to buy me a ring." She paused, glancing down at her unadorned hands. "I was going to be Mrs. Kip Hurst."

"I'm so sorry," was all I could think of to say.

"It wasn't your fault. That whole petition thing was outrageous. I couldn't believe what was going on. One of my friends tried to get me to sign it, but I refused."

"Thank you," I said sincerely. How ironic that someone who didn't know me treated me more fairly than the friend who knew me best.

"Things that aren't fair make me boil. That's why I wanted to talk to you, so you'd know that I wasn't like all those jerks. Besides if anyone is to blame, it's me." She frowned. "I let Kip down."

"You didn't. It was an accident."

"But I sent him to his death." She grew quiet and pale. "I haven't told anyone what really happened that night, but you deserve to know."

"What?"

"That it was all my . . . my fault." Her voice cracked.

"No, it wasn't," I said, gently patting her quaking shoulders. "He was speeding and lost control of his car."

"Only because he was upset because of what I did . . . or what I wouldn't do."

"What are you saying?"

She sucked in a deep breath, then slowly blew it out. "What everyone thinks is only half right. So what if we had a few drinks after the prom? I mean, who didn't? It was prom night, for Christ's sake. Most of our friends went to all-night parties, and we got invited to a few, but we wanted to be alone. So we didn't stick around to find out who made Prom King and Queen. It was gonna be the most romantic night of my life and we had all these wonderful plans . . ." Her voice cracked. "No one but me knows why Kip was driving so fast that night."

My heart revved up, but I kept my expression calm, encouraging her to go on with a sympathetic, "What happened?"

"First you have to understand about my contract."

"Contract?"

She glanced around to make sure we were completely alone, then whispered, "The chastity contract. I pledged not to have sex till marriage and signed it in front of my minister. See this ring I wear on a chain?" She lifted a gold chain with a small white ring from her neck. "Everyone who made the pledge got one of these rings. It was sacred to me, but Kip thought it was a joke."

He would, I thought.

"When we first started going out and I told him about my pledge, he was okay with it. But then we got closer and—" Her cheeks reddened. "Well, he kept pushing me to break my contract. I refused, even though I was afraid he'd dump me. But he didn't dump me—instead he asked me to marry him. That was the happiest day of my whole life. And I wanted to show him how much I cared, so I promised to tear up the contract on prom night."

I shifted uneasily in my chair, a little embarrassed. Still nothing short of a natural disaster would stop me from listening.

"All during the prom, I kept thinking about the contract, feeling guilty, and not able to enjoy myself. I was so nervous. Afterwards, Kip drove a few miles to a hotel, but I couldn't make myself get out of the car. I panicked and couldn't go through with it. He got all pissed and called me ugly names. I was crying, begging him to still love me, but he didn't say anything and just dropped me off at my house. Then he sped off without saying goodbye . . . and I never saw him alive again."

"Oh, Aileen. You didn't do anything wrong."

"Except reject the love of my life and send him to his death. That's why it was wrong for anyone to blame you. I mean, I was the guilty one."

"Kip was the one driving and at fault. Not you. Or me. I've put it behind me—you should, too."

"How can I?" She sniffled, tears shining in her dark eyes. "Don't you see? Kip was my soul mate. My perfect other half and the only guy for me."

"You'll find someone else."

"Never. I'll always love Kip."

"Oh, Aileen. You don't mean that."

"But I do. I've pledged myself to stay true to him forever." She tucked the chain back in her top, then reached out with cold fingers to touch my hand. "I will never date again."

16

Never date again? I hoped Aileen wasn't serious. But what if she was? Death had a ripple effect and could tragically hurt so many people. Life may go on, but with pieces missing.

Feeling protective of Aileen, I kept what she told me in confidence. When Dominic asked what I'd learned, I just said Aileen was still grieving for Kip.

But alone in my room, I thought over what she told me and realized something important. Aileen must be *the girl*—the one Kip wanted me to help. And now that I'd met her, I wanted to help her, too. She was too sweet to be miserable and lonely forever. I needed to convince her to get out and start living her life again. Maybe love again, too.

I didn't know how I'd accomplish this, but I'd figure out something now that I knew who Kip wanted me to help.

At least I thought I knew—until a few hours later when Amy rushed into my room and announced that she'd found out who Kip wanted me to help.

And it wasn't Aileen.

* * *

Amy sat on the edge of my bed, her legs tucked underneath her, leaning forward with an eager expression. Her long dark hair was tied back in a purple scrunchie and she wore a T-shirt with a stack of books smashing a clock and the logo, "So Many Books. So Little Time."

"Aren't you excited by what I found out?" she asked.

I could only manage a weak nod.

"I knew you'd be! I wanted to tell you last night only we got home late and you were already asleep. Then this morning you left before I even got up. Mom was yelling cause your note didn't say much. She says you have to stay put until she gets home from a church auxiliary meeting so you guys can talk."

"Just great," I said with a gulp.

"It's no big deal, only stuff about school."

"That's what worries me. Did she say which school?"

"No." Amy shook her head. "But she seems pleased with everything, so it can't be that bad."

"I hope not. So tell me more about Leanna."

"You were right to suspect her."

I remembered telling Amy that Kip's ghost asked me to help an unknown girl. At first I thought he meant Leanna. But that was before I met Aileen.

My little sister scooted closer on my bed, pushing back a loose dark curl dangling around her excited face. "Leanna's got a secret."

"What makes you think that?"

"Yesterday while Ashley and I had manicures, Leanna's mother was getting her hair permed a few chairs away and I heard major stuff."

"Eavesdropping?" I teased.

"And darned good at it." My little sister nodded proudly.

"What'd you hear?"

"Mrs. Hurst was talking loud since her head was under a dryer so it was easy to listen. Someone asked how she was doing. She said she was fine, but her daughter was still suffering. That's the word she used. Suffering."

"Suffering how?" I leaned forward eagerly.

"I don't know. Maybe she's sick."

"She didn't look sick. What else did Mrs. Hurst say?"

"Nothing about Leanna, just boring grown-up stuff." Amy flipped a dark tendril from her face. "But I can snoop around to find out—"

"Don't waste your time." I put up my hand. "Leanna isn't the right girl."

"She is too!" Amy insisted. "She's so sick, she's probably dying."

"You're just guessing. I found the girl Kip wants me to help."

"Who?"

"Kip's girlfriend. I talked to her and she's really messed up."

My sister pursed her lips. "Kip probably had lots of girlfriends, but he only had one sister. Leanna needs our help. If you don't help her, Kip's gonna be real mad at you. He'll keep haunting you forever."

"I doubt that. He has better things to do than hang around haunting me. Besides, I don't know how to help Leanna."

"Just use your powers."

"Sure. While I'm at it I'll get rid of global warming, poverty, and pollution. Seriously, I'm just a tool for communication—a phone has more powers than I do. I never know when a ghost or spirit will contact me."

"Kip talked to you because his sister is in trouble," my sister insisted.

"Not my problem."

"You have to help."

"Amy, you're impossible." I let out a weary breath. "Let's say Leanna is the right girl—what can I do?"

"That's what I'm gonna find out when I go to her—"

Amy was interrupted by a sharp knock on my door.

"Sabine, are you in there?" my mother called.

"I'll fill you in later. " Amy jumped off my bed and went over to the door and opened it. "Hi, Mom. I gotta go."

Amy disappeared down the hall as my mother strode into my room. Her expression was solemn and her arms held an ominous-looking orange folder.

"Sabine, we're going to talk," she said in a no-nonsense tone. "No more going to bed early or rushing off without letting me know what you're doing."

"I left a note."

"You call that a note? Out with a friend? What friend? Out where? And no mention of when you planned to be back."

"I didn't think you'd mind. You could have tried my cell phone."

"I did." Her eyes narrowed.

Checking my purse, I found out my phone was dead. Oops. Guess I should have recharged it.

But hardly anyone had my cell number; most of my friends preferred email.

Mom strode over to my desk and set the orange folder down. She was all business and agitated. Her determined expression spelled out trouble as she grabbed a chair, turned it around, then sat down to face me.

Instead of meeting her gaze, I noticed how her hands were folded, one elegantly overlapping the other. The diamond in her wedding ring was as large as her thumbnail, reflecting sunlight coming through my window, sending sparkles across my wall. Her nails were squared and manicured in a French style. Her skin was slightly darker and rougher than mine. And there was a tiny scar on her right knuckle, an injury from when she and Dad played couples tennis. But now they were more like two singles than a couple.

"Sabine!" she said sternly. "Would you pay attention to me? It's important we discuss your education."

Trapped, with no escape this time, I thought, fighting the panic rising in me. I eyed that thick orange folder and saw my own name scrawled across the flap. Enrollment papers, for my new school. (Or my old school?) I might as well find out what my mother had planned—even if she ended up ruining my entire life.

"Okay, tell me," I said in the same tone a death row inmate would use to find out how many days before execution. "Am I going to a private school?"

Mom shook her head, the dark blond waves so carefully arranged they didn't move. "I researched private schools, but found none of them adequate."

"Well I'm NOT going back to Arcadia High!" I exclaimed, jumping up and folding my arms across my chest. "No way. Not ever! If that's what you're going to tell me, I don't want to hear it."

"Would you sit down and act reasonably?" she asked in this calm voice that made me want to throw something at her. Didn't she realize it was my life we were discussing? She couldn't just make decisions without asking me. I wasn't ten like my sisters, I was almost an adult. I had a right to choose my own school. I'd given up a lot to move back home for her, and this was how she repaid me? By sending me back to a school where I'd be shunned and insulted and ignored?

I started to reach for my suitcase, when Mom put her hand on my arm. "Sabine, would you please listen without jumping to wrong conclusions?"

"Wrong?" I sniffed. "You said it wasn't a private school and the nearest public school is Arcadia High."

"I would never allow you to return to that narrow-minded school."

"You wouldn't?" If I hadn't been sitting down, I would have fallen over. "So what school am I going to?"

"None."

"What?" I stared at her in shock. "You're home-schooling me?"

"Me? Heaven forbid! Even if I had the time, I wouldn't have the patience." She chuckled. "I doubt either of us would survive that."

"Okay, so no Arcadia High," I said counting off with my fingers. "No private school. No home school. Guess I'm dropping out."

"Ha, ha." She frowned, not at all amused.

"Then what? What's left?"

Mom handed the orange folder to me and said, "Open it."

Uneasily, I opened the folder and pulled out bundles of papers. Assignments for English, calculus, science, Spanish, etc, all from teachers with names I recognized.

"These are *my* teachers! From Sheridan High."

"Exactly." Mom nodded.

"I don't understand," I said, wrinkling my brow.

"You would if you'd simply listen."

"I *am* listening."

"I researched all options and concluded since it's mid-semester, it would be too disruptive for you to change schools. So I made all the arrangements for independent study."

"Not a new school?"

"You won't attend school at all. Until the semester is over, and I can make better arrangements, you're still a student of Sheridan High."

17

I celebrated Mom's fantastic news by making phone calls.

First Nona, but got her machine and left a message.

Then I called Josh. We talked for over an hour. After I told him about my independent study program, he told me the latest in his life. Even small things like going to the mall to buy new sneakers sounded exciting coming from Josh. He had a natural skill for conversation and connecting with people. If he changed his mind about being a magician, he'd make a great politician. His sexy smile alone could win an election. As he described giving his dog (nicknamed Horse) a bath, I thought how lucky I was to have a boyfriend who was both funny and honest. It was silly to want anything more.

"Horse raced down the hall lathered in soap and jumped in Dad's lap," Josh went on. "Mom doubled over laughing at Dad—until he ran to her and shook his fur, showering her with bubbles."

"Your parents must have freaked."

"Nah. They thought it was funny, too. Dad even helped me drag Horse back to the bathroom."

"You're lucky your parents are so relaxed. My mother would have hit the roof. She doesn't allow pets in her house except fish."

"Your mother's not that bad. I liked her when we met at your sisters' birthday party."

"She liked you, too."

"So she has good taste," he said jokingly. "I know you don't always get along with her—"

"That's an understatement."

"But she cares about you. Give her credit for arranging independent study."

"Well . . . okay. That was cool."

"I got some cool news, too," Josh added, lowering his voice. "A great opportunity with my mentor. I'd tell you more, but Arturo swore me to secrecy. And secrecy is the core of all stage magic."

The hint of mystery and excitement in his tone amped my curiosity. I didn't mean to psychically "eavesdrop," but I had this sudden flash of a room with a long table draped with a gold cloth. There were lit candles and guys in black suits passing out cards, but it wasn't like the poker games Nona played with her friends. Maybe Tarot cards, but not like any deck I'd ever seen. They were black with gold symbols of daggers, spiders, and gargoyles. Strange and creepy. I shivered, sensing dark forces. But that was silly, right? Josh only performed cheesy magic tricks.

Shrugging this off, we talked for a while longer. Before Josh hung up, he promised to visit me on Saturday. "I swear on Horse's big doggie feet that I won't cancel," he joked.

I was still chuckling when I called Penny-Love, but she didn't notice. Before I said more than "hi," she congratulated me on the independent study problem. Was she psychic or something? I thought, then smiled to myself as she explained that she'd heard it from one of her brothers who had a girlfriend with a sister whose cousin worked in the school office.

"Woo hoo!" Penny-Love rejoiced. "It's like we're still going to school together!"

"Except you'll hang out with friends while I study here by myself."

"So it's not perfect, but at least you'll get your work done on time," she teased. "Besides, you won't be that alone. We can do homework together."

"Right," I said doubtfully. "I'll just jump in Mom's car and drive over a hundred miles to conjugate some verbs."

"I meant studying together online or the phone."

"Oh. That might work, although it won't be the same." I sighed. "I just want to move back."

"Will your parents let you?"

"I'm working on it. Mom won't want me around if I do something scandalous and embarrass her. Then she'll kick me out again."

"So scandalize ASAP and get your bad-ass back here," Penny-Love joked. "Although I can't imagine you doing anything really bad."

"You'd be surprised." I couldn't say more without revealing that I was psychic and recently talked to the ghost of the guy whose death I predicted. I liked having Penny-Love think I was normal.

So I just said I'd hooked up with some friends from my old school that my mother didn't approve of, which was mostly true. When I'd started high school, Mom had lectured me on the importance of participating in extracurricular activities. She'd suggested I join the school band (despite the fact that I couldn't play an instrument). Then when I told her I'd joined the fencing club, she was not pleased. "Too violent," she disapproved. I tried to explain the artistic and mental benefits of fencing, but she wasn't interested.

Whenever Dad and my sisters attended my Foils exhibitions, Mom was always busy. Coincidence? Doubtful. I'd never meet my mother's expectations, so why even try?

"Well I hope you move back soon," Penny-Love was saying.

"That's my goal. I'll embarrass Mom so badly, she'll pack my bags for me."

Penny-Love laughed loudly. "I miss having you around and I know Nona does, too."

I paused and asked, "How is Nona?"

"Okay . . . well most of the time . . . oh, my other line's beeping. It must be Jacques. Did I tell you how great he is?"

"Only a zillion times. But what about Nona?"

"Nothing to worry about. Anyone could mix up cherry tomatoes for strawberries. She's fine, really. Gotta go!" Then the phone clicked off.

I stared at the phone, worries mounting. Had Nona put cherry tomatoes in a pie or strawberries in a green salad? Were her memory lapses happening more often?

Quickly, I punched Nona's number, only I got her machine. Frustrated, I left a message, then knitted while I waited for her to call back.

But she never did.

* * *

First thing in the morning, I tried Nona's number again—and nearly dropped the phone with relief when she answered.

"Nona! I was so worried, why didn't you call me back?"

"I did," she replied.

"When?" I thought back and drew a blank.

"Don't you remember, Sabine? You told me all about your sleepover."

"Sleepover?" I rubbed my forehead in confusion." Am I missing something?"

"A lot of sleep, I'd guess." She chuckled. "It can't be comfortable sleeping in a treehouse. But you and your friend seem to enjoy it."

"Friend? What friend?"

"Are you pulling my leg? You only have one best friend—Brianne."

"Brianne?" My mouth went dry, and I felt sick inside.

"Such a sweet girl and so spunky! Nothing that girl won't try at least once, like the time she strung a rope from the house to the garage and tight-roped across it. Instead of screaming, she laughed when she fell and landed in the azalea bushes. Reminds me of myself at that age."

"But Nona . . ." I took a deep breath. "Brianne isn't my friend anymore."

"You girls have a spat?"

"It's been over six months since I went on a sleepover with her. Penny-Love is my closest friend now. And I didn't talk with you yesterday. I left messages on your machine, only you never called back."

"I see." The small words echoed shame.

"It's all right, Nona," I assured.

"No, it isn't." There was a painful pause. "My thoughts are a bit muddled. I think I'll go lie down."

"You shouldn't be alone," I said firmly. "I'm going to tell Mom right now that you need me and I'm moving back."

"Don't be ridiculous. I'm far from alone. Through a window I can see Dominic carrying hay to the horses and Penny-Love will be here after school. Besides, isn't this your first day of independent study?"

"Yes," I admitted, surprised how quickly she'd snapped back to her usual self. She even remembered Penny-Love.

"Then you should start on your assignments," she ordered. "I'll talk to you later. Bye, dear." The phone clicked in my ear.

I just sat on my bed, staring around the room filled with pieces of my childhood. A bean bag pillow, a floppy stuffed unicorn that Dad won for me at a county fair, an embroidered satin jewelry box full of costume jewelry I used to share with Brianne, and a shelf of "Tea Cups Around the World" that my Grandma Rose gave me every birthday. Fragments of memories that made up who I was.

Would Nona still be Nona when her memories faded?

She'd put on a good front, waving away my worries, but it was clear she was getting worse. I was tempted to call Dominic or Penny-Love and tell them about Nona's latest memory lapse. But I kept hearing the pride in my grandmother's voice, and I had to respect her dignity.

Besides I also had to start school.

*   *   *

Getting ready for school had never been easier. I slipped into a comfy T-shirt, sweat pants, and fuzzy slippers. No makeup, fussing over my hair, deciding on clothes, or gulping down a rushed breakfast. No teachers or other students.Only me.

My family was off early, so I was the only one home. In the kitchen, I turned on the radio to an energetic hip-hop station, spiked the volume high, and ate a breakfast of cold cereal. Then I tackled my packet of papers and textbooks.

What to do first? I pondered. I looked at my list of assignments, deciding I'd pretend I was at

Sheridan High and do them in the order of my actual classes. But English was first, and I wasn't in the mood to read *The Great Gatsby*. So I poured another bowl of Cinnamon Crunch cereal and watched a game show on TV. This reminded me of being a little kid and staying home sick with Mom, before she got a social life and only worked part-time jobs. We'd watch game shows and guess the answers. A few times I knew the answers before the questions were even asked.

Somehow two hours passed, and I still hadn't completed any of my many assignments. Independent study wouldn't be as easy as I thought. I had to get serious and stop wasting time.

So I flipped through the assignments again. I even did a few math equations, only I wasn't sure I was doing them properly, and put them aside for later. I still wasn't ready to tackle Gatsby and my science assignment involved collecting dead bug specimens.

"I know what I can do!" I snapped my fingers and slammed the textbooks shut. "This is supposed to be like actual school, and every Monday I help Manny with his *Mystic Manny* column."

Then I realized I was talking to myself. Talking to spirits and even ghosts was okay, but talking to myself was one step on the road to crazy.

A short time later I'd come up with a few predictions for Manny.

Left-handed people will meet someone right for them.

Monday is a good day for money-making opportunities.

Purple is the lucky color of the week, and ten and two are lucky numbers.

Then I randomly picked someone from the yearbook for the "Ten Years in the Future" column. A junior named Austin Charles. He'd get a scholarship to an East Coast college, but would change his major midway, take an internship at an architect firm, and meet his future wife at an office party. I saw a shadow of a health problem ahead for him, but didn't include this when I emailed the column to Manny.

"Hey, Sis! Wait till you hear what I did today!" Amy exclaimed, holding her backpack as she appeared in my bedroom doorway. "And why are you still wearing slippers and a nightie? Didn't you get dressed?"

"Oops. Guess I forgot." I glanced down. "I've been busy."

"Doing homework?"

"Well . . . sort of." I avoided looking at my packet of assignments. Except for a few math problems, I hadn't done anything. And I doubted "making up" psychic predictions for the school newspaper would impress my teachers.

"Wait till you hear about my day." Grinning, Amy flopped in a chair beside me. "Guess where I'm going this evening?"

I shrugged."Where?"

"I said guess."

"I have no idea. Just tell me."

"Leanna's house."

"Kip's sister! But I thought she never invited anyone over." I wrinkled my brow. "How did you get her to change her mind?"

"She didn't. Her mother invited me."

Amy went on to explain that while Leanna's mother was volunteering to be a room mother, they got to talking. "I knew Leanna only got a C in spelling and I got an A, so I said I'd help her study. Next thing I know, Mrs. Hurst invites me over and even offers to pay me like a real tutor."

"Cool." I gestured a thumbs-up. "So when do you start?"

"After dinner. I'll help her like Kip asked."

"It's Aileen who needs help," I corrected. "Not Leanna."

Amy's long dark hair swished as she shook her head. "That's what you think."

"That's what I *know*. Kip didn't use all his energy to come here just to help his sister do better in school."

"Why not?"

"It's just the way spirits work."

"Why do you always act like you know everything and I don't know anything?" Amy demanded, her blue eyes blazing. "You're just like Ashley and Mom, never taking anything I say seriously. Don't you care what I think?"

"Of course."

"But you don't believe anything I say."

"I know you wouldn't lie. I just think differently."

"Differently means you think I'm wrong. Well you're the one who's wrong." She glared at me. "And I'm going to prove it!"

18

Bad moods are toxic and spread like noxious mold.

About an hour later, I was nuking a frozen lasagna in the microwave when hurricane Ashley stormed into the kitchen. Amy trailed after her, looking miserable.

"Sabine, where's Mom?" Ashley asked, flipping her long dark hair over her shoulder and looking around. "I want to tell her what's going on. Amy just told me she was invited to Leanna's house. It's not fair!"

I shrugged, gesturing that my mouth was full of lasagna. I chewed slowly to avoid getting involved. I pretended not to notice the "help me" look Amy tossed in my direction.

"Ashley, it's no big deal," Amy insisted. "I'm just tutoring Leanna."

"Then I want to tutor, too."

"You suck at spelling. You only got a C on your last test."

"C plus!"

"Can you spell curious, opposite, reflection, or challenge?"

"Doesn't matter. I'm still going with you."

"You weren't invited."

"Leanna is *my* best friend!"

"Then why hasn't she ever invited *you* over?"

"Maybe her house is a mess or smells bad. I don't even care, I just want to go there. There's no way you get to and not me."

I thought Ashley was acting like a spoiled brat, but I knew better than to take sides. Besides I felt a little guilty, wondering if I was part of the reason Ashley hadn't been welcome in her best friend's house. So I said nothing and sat quietly at the table, eating lasagna.

Mom showed up a few minutes later, though, and she had plenty to say. She bristled with indignation like she'd been personally insulted. Soon she was on the phone talking to Mrs. Hurst. When she hung up she wore a triumphant look, and announced that they were all going to the Hurst house.

Of course "all" didn't include me, and no one suggested I go along. I understood why, yet found myself feeling a bit like Cinderella being left behind while her sisters dashed off to the ball.

A short while later, they were gone. Dad was still at his office (as usual).

I thought how ironic it was that Mom had invited me back so I could be a part of our family. But what family? I was here alone; stranded on an island called home.

Feeling aimless, I searched the freezer until I found a quart of French vanilla ice cream. I usually resisted emotional eating, but now I didn't care. So I settled into a leather recliner in the living room and kept switching channels, not sure what to watch. The house seemed big and empty when no one else was around. I never felt lonely at Nona's house, even when she wasn't there.

And Dominic is always close by, too, I thought. Then despite the cool ice cream in my mouth, I felt hot all over. I quickly shut off those thoughts.

I knew I should do my school assignments. But I started thinking about Kip, having a sense he was nearby although I couldn't see him. Was his energy fading? I wondered.

He'd given me his message. Now I just had to figure it out.

Despite Amy's theory about Leanna, I was positive Kip wanted me to help Aileen. She'd never be happy if she didn't get over his death. She needed a new guy in her life; someone who wouldn't propose just to break her chastity contract. Because I was sure that's what Kip did.

So how to help Aileen?

But how could I find the right guy for her? I was far from an expert in romance, muddling through my own relationship with massive amounts of confusion. I needed to get some advice from a professional.

Fortunately, I knew one.

"Of course!" I snapped my fingers. "Soul-Mate Matches."

Calling for matchmaking tips would accomplish two things: checking up on Nona and helping Aileen. Asking for Nona's assistance would also give me an excuse (without offending her pride) to see how she's doing. I still felt uneasy after Nona's failing memory. How could she think Brianne was still my best friend? It was like her mind short-circuited, making her think she was living in the past.

Before I could call my grandmother, the phone rang.

Not Nona, I knew as reached for the phone. Someone older than me that I respected, a person of authority, a teacher . . .

"Good afternoon, Sabine," Mr. Landreth greeted.

I knew immediately what this was about, and I almost laughed at my former teacher's persistence. He was determined to bring me back into fencing by having me assist his beginner's class. That job would mean dealing with annoying kids like Kevin and also answering the same beginner-type questions over and over. It would require loads of patience.

I listened while my former teacher listed reasons why I should work for him. He told me I was responsible, helpful, and talented. He even offered a very attractive wage to tempt me. I let him go on for a bit, enjoying the compliments. He made it sound like I'd be doing him a big favor if I just agreed to assist a few hours a week.

But really he was the one doing me the favor.

I looked around at the empty room, where the only sound came from the hum of the refrigerator. I made a bitter face at the thick folder full of school assignments. I really, really wasn't in the mood for homework. I needed to be around people, to keep active, to get my mind off problems and do something interesting.

So I accepted the job.

I had no idea I'd just put myself in the path of danger, and by this evening, something terrible would happen.

19

In one corner of the room, beginners lined up against a wall, decked out in bulky, protective canvas suits and waving sabers. That's where I was supposed to focus, but my attention kept wandering to the elite group on the other side of the room.

When I'd arrived and saw the members of Foils practicing, I tried to act cool like I hardly noticed them. I gave a casual wave at Vin. He lifted his saber and shouted out "Hey, Sabine!"

I waved back, glad he was over being mad at me for not answering his questions about Brianne. Not that I had any answers. I had no clue what was up with that girl. Her whole Jekyll and Hyde freak show confused me. Before Kip's death we'd been so close, then suddenly she hated me for no obvious reason.

Brianne's loss, I told myself. But her betrayal still cut deep and my gaze drifted in her direction.

Damn her anyway, I thought angrily as I spotted her across the room. If she hadn't signed that petition, I'd still be in Foils. I could have endured the cruel rumors and even stood up to my mother if I'd had Brianne's support. But when she turned against me, I just didn't care enough to fight. The real reason I'd left town and started over wasn't because of the rumors, but because I'd lost my best friend.

Even decked out in bulky protective gear, she looked more fragile than I remembered. But her fencing style was still bold and aggressive. She preferred to attack, seldom taking the defensive role. In a way, this made her an easier opponent because

I could guess what she would do next. In fencing, anyway. Not when it came to friendship.

Brianne's fencing moves had improved, so much, I wondered if I could still beat her. She'd developed stronger defense skills; sidestepping and jumping back when I expected her to lunge forward. She played with intensity, advancing on her opponent, Tony, like she was fighting in a life-or-death battle.

Other Foil members paired off for practice, too. Vin parried with Alphonso; and Jennae with a pony-tailed guy I didn't recognize, although he resembled Derrick's opponent so I guessed they were brothers. There was a tall auburn-haired girl who stood off to the side, and I wondered if it was Annika.

I heard someone call my name and turned to find Mr. Landreth heading my way. A small boy followed him and I groaned when I recognized Kevin's pesky grin.

Once class started, I did my best to ignore the advanced fencing on the far end of the room while I worked on basics with beginners. The best part was when Mr. Landreth and I paired off for a short demonstration. The beginners applauded, clearly impressed, which gave me a boost of confidence.

Afterwards I worked individually with the students, showing how to hold their saber, bend their knees, and move forward and back. One woman seemed afraid of her saber, so I poked my arm with the rubber tip to show that it didn't hurt. A girl a few years younger than me kept trying to twirl her saber like a baton until I threatened to take it away. And an older man complained that his glove was too tight. Then there was hyper Kevin who kept piling me with questions and never waiting for my answer. I managed to keep my cool, proud to discover I possessed a lot of patience. And with Kevin, I sorely needed a lot of patience!

When we had our first ten-minute break, Kevin dumped his sword and helmet by the wall, then trailed after me like an energetic puppy.

I sat down at the table where I'd left my bottle of iced tea. I turned my back on Kevin, hoping he'd get the hint. Instead, he circled around and sat next to me.

"Hiya, Sabine."

"Kevin, this is a break so I can rest," I told him.

"Can I wear your glove?" he asked. "How come your glove is purple while mine is red? Where did you get that fancy helmet? Did it cost a lot? My helmet isn't shiny like yours."

"You're getting rented equipment for free, so be happy with what you got."

"Can I rent your helmet?"

"No," I said firmly.

"Your cool glove?"

"No."

"Will you be my partner?"

"Isn't Marsha your partner?"

"She tripped and got mad at me."

"Why did she get mad at you?"

"I tied her shoelaces together."

I almost said something I'd regret. Instead, I took a sip of iced tea and prayed for patience. He was just a little boy and shouting at him might feel good but it wouldn't be very mature.

"Please, please be my partner!" he persisted.

"Oh, all right. But no more tying shoelaces," I told him firmly.

Then before he could ask more questions, I went into the only place I was sure he wouldn't follow me. The restroom.

As I pushed in the door, someone on the other side pushed out. I stepped back and the door slid open. And there facing me was the last person I expected to see.

Brianne looked even more shocked than I felt.

"What are you doing here?" she gasped.

"I think that's obvious," I said calmly. But I didn't feel calm inside, and it took a lot of energy to act natural. I'd imagined this scene for six months, going over all the witty and sarcastic things I'd say to her. Only now I couldn't think of even one. And a traitorous part of me actually felt happy to see my ex-best friend.

But she was far from happy. "You're following me!" she accused.

"Following you?" I was so stunned by this accusation that I could hardly speak. "That's crazy! I had no idea you were in the bathroom."

"You're lying! I know you've been watching me. Every time I look up, you're staring at me, like you're trying to read my mind. Stop it!"

"Brianne, you're paranoid."

"Just leave me alone."

Instead of anger, I felt pity. This was not the same confident Brianne I used to know. What had happened to her?

"Brianne, are you okay?"

She didn't reply, instead her gaze swept the room as if looking for escape. I had the weird impression that she was afraid of me. An invisible barrier of volatile energy sizzled between us. For a frozen moment, we stood without saying anything. And in her golden brown aura, I sensed regret. Was she sorry for how she treated me? Did she miss the close friendship we'd had?

"Is there anything you'd like to tell me?" I persisted.

"No! I have to get back to Tony," she said, not meeting my gaze. "He'll wonder what's taking so long."

"And I wonder what you're doing with him."

"Isn't it obvious?" She lifted her shoulders defiantly. "He's my boyfriend."

"But the last I heard you weren't interested in him."

"I'm way interested. He's wild about me and treats me like a princess."

I summoned a smile. "Well, that's cool. I'm happy for you."

"Then why are you smiling in that fake way?"

I stopped smiling, surprised she could still read me so well. "I just never figured Tony for your type. He's too rough around the edges."

"He's perfect for me and we're doing great together."

"We used to be great together," I said sadly. "What happened?"

She glanced down, her hand gripping the door handle white-knuckled, but didn't answer.

"You were my friend . . . my best friend." My words were a painful whisper. "Just tell me . . . Why?"

Her eyes clouded over and she shook her head.

"And you went ahead and got the tattoo . . . our faery tattoo."

"I didn't need your permission." Her tone sharpened and she glared at me. "Back off, Sabine. I mean it—stay out of my life or you'll be sorry."

She reached for the door, but I couldn't just let her go. A voice in my head was saying "talk to her," and I felt a desperate urgency. I grabbed for her arm, my fingers digging through her canvas jacket.

"Let go!" She jerked her arm back, cradling it against her chest as my touch had burned her. With a furious glare, she jerked open the door with her other arm and slammed out of the room.

I could hear Opal's voice in my head telling me to go after her.

She's hurting . . . she needs you, my spirit guide insisted.

"She hates me," I thought back.

Hate is a double-edged emotion.

"I can't make her talk to me."

You limit your own abilities and do not realize your potential for discovery.

"I discovered enough already. I give up."

There was a sigh and I could tell Opal had given up with me, too.

Just as well, I told myself. I didn't need a toxic person like Brianne in my life. I'd been dumb opening up to her, like a burn victim rushing back into a fire. I should have just walked away without saying anything.

Yet there had been a moment—a brief flicker of the old Brianne and Sabine combo. Had I imagined it? I didn't think so, yet now that it was over, I wasn't so sure. And what did it matter anyway?

Sighing, I went back to the table, sat down, and sipped tea while looking around the room. I saw that Kevin had switched targets and was now hopping all around Mr. Landreth. The break was almost over and Alphonso, Derrick, and Vin were heading back to the floor. Brianne was already there with Tony, smiling up at him like he was her dream guy instead of a chauvinistic jock. She stood on her tiptoes to curl her arms around Tony's massive shoulders. He leaned down and planted a smooshy one on her, which seemed tacky considering little kids were around. But the lovely-dovey duo didn't care.

Yeah, Brianne didn't care. Not about me anyway—and I'd have to accept it.

Watching them gave me a bitter taste in my mouth, or maybe my iced tea was too warm. The break ended and Kevin raced over to me.

"You're my partner," he reminded.

I groaned, then told him to put back on his helmet and get his saber.

Nearby I caught Mr. Landreth's gaze and he gave me a thumbs-up gesture. Then Kevin returned, waving his sword around.

"Stand on that line," I told him. "And put your saber down until I say 'ready.'"

Surprisingly, he did what I asked.

Then I stepped back and faced him. "Hold your wrist higher and bend your knees more."

He nodded, bending his knees and lifting his wrist.

"Much better," I approved.

"So can I hit you now?" he asked too eagerly.

"Almost." I adjusted my helmet so my face was protected, bent my knees, and lifted my saber. "Ready. Fence."

Then I moved forward, planning to take the offense and show Kevin how to defend himself. Only Kevin ran forward, forgetting to keep his saber raised so that it was pointing downward.

"Lift up with your—" I started, only Kevin waved the saber wildly and I felt a jab in my leg.

"I'm sorry!" Kevin yelped, dropping his saber so it clattered to the floor.

I started to say that it was okay, he couldn't really hurt me with a blunted saber tip, but my leg burned with a hot stinging sensation. When I looked down at my gray fencing pants, I saw a jagged slash in the fabric.

And something red dripped down my leg.

Blood.

20

Kevin started crying and begging me not to be angry.

"I didn't mean to," he sobbed.

"I know you didn't," I said, bending over to cover the flow with my ungloved hand. "Go get Mr. Landreth. Hurry!"

Kevin tossed his saber aside and took off running.

My leg stung but wasn't really painful; mostly I felt surprise. Rented swords were always blunted. But when I looked at Kevin's saber, I saw the blade had been broken and sharpened to a pointed tip.

A tip now tinged with my blood.

How could this happen? My former teacher had always checked and double-checked the equipment, making sure it was completely safe. The only injuries I'd gotten while fencing were bruises and pulled muscles.

"Sabine, what's wrong?" Mr. Landreth asked, coming over. As his gaze rested on my leg, his eyes widened. "Ohmygod!"

"I stabbed her," Kevin cried. "But it was an accident. Honest."

"Of course, it was," I assured, blood dripping between my fingers. "While I clean up, take a look at Kevin's saber. Okay? Something isn't right."

"That's for damn sure," Mr. Landreth said, reaching for Kevin's saber. As he studied the blade, his brows raised, but we couldn't talk with the students gathering around.

A few Foils members noticed the commotion, too. When Jennae came over and saw my injury, she gave a shrill cry, then hustled me off to the rest-room. She dug through a cabinet until she found some antiseptic and helped me clean and bandage my wound . . . She was so good at watching out for everyone.

"Does it hurt?" she asked, closing the box of bandages.

"Not much."

"How come you didn't notice Kevin had a sharp saber?"

"It all happened quickly. I guess I wasn't pay-ing attention."

"So how come no one checked the equipment? Mr. Landreth is usually so careful."

"Kevin was probably messing around and dam-aged it. And that's not all that's damaged." I glanced ruefully at my favorite pair of fencing pants. To clean my injury, we'd had to rip them so now they were lopsided; one stretchy leg to my ankle and the other ragged below my knee.

"Didn't you special order them from *Cutlass Creations*?" Jennae asked.

"Yeah, and they fit perfectly," I added with a sigh. "Now they're ruined."

"Bad luck is following you around. All those rumors at school about your having freaky powers that caused that football player's car to crash and then getting expelled. Of course I knew it wasn't true, but everything happens for a reason, and it seemed like fate was trying to tell you something."

There was an odd note in her tone, and I stiffened. "Like what?"

"I don't know . . ."

"What are you trying hard not to say?"

"Well . . . maybe you shouldn't have moved back." She shrugged. "I mean, I think it's great you're here and I'd love to have you in Foils again. But is it worth it if bad things happen? I don't want you to get hurt."

"Nothing's going to happen to me."

"I hope so." Pushing her bangs from her solemn eyes, she frowned at my leg. "Be careful and watch your back." Turning abruptly, she left the room.

Following her, I watched her cross the floor to join the new girl Annika. They whispered intently, Annika glancing over at me.

I turned away so I wouldn't be caught staring, and started for the beginner's area. Class was taking a break, and I noticed Kevin sitting by himself in a folding chair. His shoulders drooped unhappily as he stared down at the floor. I was about to go over and talk to him, when Mr. Landreth called me into his office.

"Sabine," he said in a grave tone. His brows creased as he stared at the saber in his hands. "I can't begin to express how terribly sorry I am about this. I take full responsibility."

"I'm okay. Really," I assured.

"See this mark?" Turning the saber over, he pointed to an X–slash of red paint on the hilt. "This saber was put away in a cabinet with other unsafe equipment. I never would have offered it to students."

"How did Kevin get it?"

"Beats me. When I asked him, he said it wasn't his usual saber. He seemed to think someone took his while he was on break, but it's more likely he grabbed the wrong one by mistake." He gave a grim shake of his head. "Only how did this saber get out of the cabinet?"

"Someone must have taken it by mistake."

"Mistakes aren't acceptable. I'll ask around and get to the bottom of this," Mr. Landreth decided with a creased brow. Then he told me to go on home for the night, promising to pay me for the full time. I argued that I could stay until class ended, but he said he wanted to insure I made it home safely.

"Safely?" I rolled my eyes. "It's just a cut. No big deal."

"It's a big deal to me. Humor me and allow your friends to escort you home."

"Friends?" For a confused moment I thought of Penny-Love, Josh, Thorn, and Dominic. But they were as far away as a past life.

Mr. Landreth opened the door, ushering Vin and Alphonso inside. They had suited down into their regular clothes; Vin in a striped silky shirt over a blue tee with black denim jeans and Alphonso in baggy jeans with a black T-shirt boosting a fiery dragon design.

"Must you work so hard to be the center of attention?" Vin half-joked, wagging his finger at me.

"This wasn't my idea."

"Does it hurt?"

"Not really. And it's not bleeding anymore, so you guys don't have to baby-sit me. Go back to fencing."

"We've practiced enough," Vin said. "We'll be back every night this week getting ready for Saturday's gig at the Renaissance Fair. Gonna come watch us?"

"Can't. I've already made some plans with my boyfriend." I was glad to have an honest reason to refuse. Watching Foils instead of performing with them would feel weird.

Alphonso shifted in his giant-sized sneakers. "Br—bring him."

"Maybe some other time," I said evasively. No way did I want Josh around my old friends.

Vin swooped down and picked up my equipment bag. "Let's roll."

"I can carry my own bag. Do my arms look broken? Would you stop fussing over me already."

"Not a chance," Vin joked. "I've missed giving you a bad time."

I should have been annoyed, but Vin's heart was in the right place. And Alphonso's kindness came through his actions rather than words. I wouldn't admit it to them, but their concern meant a lot to me. It was almost like the six months apart had never happened and I was still part of the group.

"Here's what we're gonna do," Vin said in his typical bossy-Vin attitude. "I'll drive you in your car and Alphonso will follow in his car and pick me up after I make sure you're okay."

"I am okay, how many times do I have to tell you? I can drive myself home."

"I know, but we promised Mr. L," Vin insisted. "Now no arguments."

Alphonso's 80's Toyota Corolla was parked beside my mother's car. I glanced through the grimy windows and saw what looked like a fast-food disaster. Soda cans, candy wrappers, food containers, and papers were scattered everywhere. He had to push aside some graphic novels and a Dungeons and Dragons handbook to sit down in the front seat.

Vin followed me to my car and seemed to think he was going to drive until I set him straight. Once he was fastened in the passenger seat, I hit the gas and cranked up my radio.

A short while later I pulled into the driveway and thanked the guys for watching out for me. Then I ducked through the garage entrance, wanting to avoid any awkward questions about my bandaged leg and bloody pants. I heard the TV on in the living room and the murmur of voices as I headed upstairs. Climbing stairs loosened my bandage and I felt the wet trickle of blood dripping down.

In the bathroom, I sorted through the medicine cabinet for antiseptic, cringing at the stinging pain as I put on a new bandage.

The jagged cut wasn't deep, but swollen and red. Even after it healed, it would probably leave a scar. How had a damaged saber ended up with the rental equipment anyway? According to Kevin someone had switched his saber. But why would anyone do that? There was no way of being sure who Kevin would pair off with since we randomly changed partners.

Maybe not so random tonight, I realized with a sickening feeling.

Kevin had shouted that he wanted me for his next partner. Then he'd set down his equipment and went on break. No one was watching his saber and anyone could have picked it up.

I didn't like where these thoughts were headed, but facts added up to an ugly suspicion.

Had my accident been accidental?

Or a deliberate attempt to hurt me?

21

I dreamed about swords and faceless fencers.

A menacing figure in a helmet, his or her face hidden, juggled sabers, tossing them higher and higher into the air, until they started spinning by themselves. A cyclone of swords swirled around me, their tips sharpening with each twirl like a pencil spinning in a pencil sharpener. They grew large and blended into one giant sword, its tip dripping with blood, and with evil eyes glaring from the silvery hilt. The eyes targeted me and the giant blade zoomed closer and closer.

Gasping for air, I sat up in bed, relieved to be in one piece and safe underneath warm blankets. For a moment the dream lingered, and I felt vulnerable, peering around nervously. My dream wasn't a premonition, but rather a warning.

Someone was out to get me.

I hugged my knees to my chest under my covers and stared around my room as if enemies lurked in shadowed corners. My sun-shaped nightlight gave my room soft yellow illumination, but my thoughts drifted in darkness.

It was hard to believe someone there last night had maliciously targeted me. Maybe it wasn't personal, but a dumb prank. Yeah, that made more sense. Although who could be dumb enough to switch a safe saber with a sharp one? It could have resulted in serious injury. I was just glad Kevin hadn't stabbed himself. He may be an annoying pain-in-the-butt, but I didn't want to see him hurt.

So back to the big question: Who switched the sabers? It had to have been someone who could handle the equipment without attracting attention; someone who knew where Mr. Landreth kept defective equipment; and someone with a grudge against me.

A name popped in my mind, but I pushed it away.

Impossible.

But who else?

Brianne clearly didn't want me around and acted like she hated me. Maybe she hoped to scare me away. Only why do something so risky instead of just asking me to leave? Nothing made sense. Brianne had her faults; she could be impulsive and irresponsible, but she'd never been cruel. And once upon our friendship, I would have trusted her with my life.

Now all trust was gone.

Still it couldn't be Brianne. So I ran through a mental list of everyone at the fencing center last night, starting with the most unlikely candidate— Mr. Landreth. To be impartial, he did have ample opportunity. The damaged saber was kept in his office, so it would be easy for him to make the switch. But the last thing he'd want would be an injury during his class. If someone had been seriously hurt he could have had to shut down. So he was definitely *not* a suspect.

What about his fencing students? I'd never met any of them before this class and only knew their first names. So there was no motive—unless there was an unknown connection that made one of them my enemy. The students had plenty of opportunity to switch sabers. But they had no business going into Mr. Landreth's office, so that would be risky. Besides, how would a new student know about old equipment stowed away in a cabinet?

That left the Foils: old friends, new members—and Brianne.

Why did my thoughts keep circling back to her?

Well I refused to suspect her. Years of friendship and trust might not matter to her, but they did to me. Screw the unanswered questions. As far as I was concerned, my accident was just that.

No one was to blame.

I glanced out the window at the gray, dreary morning, I couldn't decide whether it was too early to get up or too late to go back to sleep. Damp autumn chilled the air, making the idea of crawling back under my covers all the more tempting.

Yawning, I leaned my head against my pillow, then jumped with a start at a loud THUMP from the next room.

Had Amy fallen out of her bed?

Tossing off my blankets, I grabbed a long flannel robe and rushed to Amy's room.

I didn't waste time with polite knocking, especially when I heard a muffled groan. Yanking open the door, I saw two skinny legs poking up from underneath the bed.

"Amy? What are you doing?"

"Ouch!" My sister wiggled out on her stomach, then swiveled around to look up at me, rubbing her head.

"You're supposed to sleep in your bed, not under it," I said, kneeling beside her on the carpet.

"I wasn't sleeping, I was looking." She pulled on her green T-shirt nightie and pushed her tangled dark brown hair from her face. "You made me hit my head."

"Excuse me for being worried when I hear weird noises coming from here. What were you doing under the bed?"

"I told you—looking." She pushed herself up to her feet. "For my book."

"Only one book?" I gestured around to the crowded shelves overflowing books.

"My science book. I fell asleep reading and it slipped behind my bed."

"I'll help you find it," I offered. Then we both got on each side of the queen-sized bed and shoved it away from the wall. She reached down easily and plucked up the heavy textbook.

"Thanks," she said, sounding less grumpy now.

"No problem." I sat on a chair and asked her about last night. "How'd it go at Leanna's house? Learn anything?"

"Boy, did I!" She leaned forward on the edge of her bed. "I solved everything."

"Everything, huh?" I didn't quite believe this, but she had my curiosity now.

"Wait till you hear." Her blue eyes sparkled as she launched into her story.

"I was wrong about the house being messy or smelling bad. It's just a normal house, really big, with fancy artwork and lots of fake flowers. While the adults talked, Ashley and Leanna whispered and I couldn't hear what they were saying. So I asked Leanna if we could go to her room so I could tutor her. But she weirded out and said no one was allowed in her room."

"Did she say why?"

My sister shook her head. "Her mom acted funny, too, the way grown-ups do when they don't want to answer questions. She told us to study in the game room. Only Leanna didn't want to study, and she and Ashley played computer games. They were really into the newest Sim City and forgot about me. So I said I was going to the bathroom, but really I snooped around."

"Good job, Sherlock." I high-fived her. "What did you find?"

"Leanna's room. She had this cutesy plaque with her name on the door, so I knew I had the right place. It wasn't even locked. When I looked inside, I found her secret."

"What?" I asked eagerly.

"Her room is all about her brother. The walls are covered with pictures, letters, birthday cards and even his report cards—mostly C's if you want to know. There's this round table, too, in the center with candles around Kip's framed photo."

"A shrine?"

"Yeah, that's what you call it."

"So that's why her mother said she was suffering," I said with a sympathetic shake of my head. "She can't get over Kip's death."

"It's more than that—she's obsessed. I read one of the letters and it was from Leanna to Kip. Dated *after* he died. She wrote the same line over and over, 'I'm sorry I was bad.' But Leanna never does anything bad. All the teachers love her and she's super good at everything."

"Maybe she's trying hard to be good because she feels guilty," I said with sudden insight. It was one of those moments where I had a feeling Opal was putting thoughts into my head. Kip must have gotten mad at Leanna and told her she was "bad." Then he died before they could work things out and her last memory of him was anger. So she compensated by being Miss Perfect.

"I told you Leanna was the right girl and now I proved it," Amy said, folding her arms across her chest.

"She needs professional counseling. I don't know how to help her."

"But I do."

I groaned. "I don't want to hear this."

"It'll be really cool. But you'll need to get some things while I'm at school."

I was tempted to point out that I was technically in school too, even if I didn't leave the house. Still, I was curious. "What things?"

"Snakeroot, chicory, dandelion, seven orange candles, and a black bowl."

"What for?"

"A forgiveness ceremony."

"Huh? I never heard of that."

"You should read more. I found it in this book called *Mysteries of Ancient Herbs* that I bought to give to Nona. I was skimming it when I got my idea."

"What idea?" I said uneasily.

"Elementary, my dear sister." She flashed a mischievous grin. "Leanna already thinks you're a witch. So you're gonna hex her—with black magic."

22

My little sister was crazy.

Certifiably, irrevocably, absolutely crazy.

I knew better than to mess with dark powers.
Nona and most of her friends believed in magic
spells and potions, and took it very seriously. Nona
warned never to make light of anyone else's beliefs
because believing creates truth. She taught me to
invoke white light and ask for a protection against

dark spirits when connecting with the other side. I hadn't experienced dark entities until a few weeks ago when I'd brought home an antique witch ball. I'd survived a scary encounter with a deranged ghost and was lucky to be alive.

But I couldn't always count on being lucky.

Amy was grinning like she was buckling up for a super thrilling carnival ride. "It'll be fun!" she exclaimed.

"Be serious, Amy. Leanna will never fall for this."

"Yes, she will. When she found out I'd seen her room, she was mad at first but then we got to talking and she told me about this argument she had with Kip before he died. She borrowed his football jersey and spilled a soda on it, and he blew up and yelled that she was a bad girl and he'd never forgive her."

"Then he died," I finished sadly. "No wonder Leanna is messed up."

"You can help with a forgiveness spell."

"There is no such thing. Besides, isn't she afraid of me?"

"Yes—that's why this will work. She really believes you can hex people."

"And why would I want to encourage that delusional thinking?"

"Because it's a good plan."

"Where am I supposed to get snakeroot and chicory?"

"We're not *really* casting a spell. Any weeds or leaves will fool Leanna."

There were a million arguments against this, but I'd already hurt Amy's feeling once by not taking her seriously and didn't want to do it again. So I said maybe. Somehow this translated to yes. And she hugged me so hard that she bumped against my injured leg and I had to grit my teeth so she wouldn't know I was hurt.

After breakfast, I sat down at my computer and did a search on chicory and snakeroot. I checked herbal stores and located one only a few blocks away. I also read my email and found nine messages from Penny-Love, one from Jill, a raunchy joke from Caitlyn, and Thorn passed on a chain letter about an anti-environmental senator.

As I was reading Penny-Love's third email (another chatty news flash about the wonders of Jacques), my computer made a buzzing sound then flickered on and off.

I swore and muttered, "Power surge." Then I powered down as a precaution, and waited for the screen to go dark.

Only it continued to glow, an eerie crimson-gold.

I gripped the edge of my chair and leaned forward, my heart pumping fast. This wasn't like any power surge I'd ever seen. The buzzing grew louder and the screen flamed with heat like a blazing sunset. Black lines slashed across the golden screen, racing and curving, connecting to form a foggy, yet eerily familiar face.

Turn away, I told myself. Run out of the room.

But I sat, mesmerized by this computer freak show. Dark brows over skull-like eyes and a bony nose with thin lips stretched to whisper, "Help her."

"Kip?" I whispered back. "Is that you?"

Hollow skull eyes rose up, then down, as if nodding.

"Thank goodness you came back!" I said with a sigh of relief. "I've been trying to do what you want, but I need more information."

His sunk-in mouth moved soundlessly.

"What are you trying to say?"

The disembodied head moved sideways, then sank down, until Kip vanished.

"Don't go yet! Come back!" I slapped the side of my computer. The screen flickered bright, then flashed off to darkness.

The computer seemed as dead as Kip was supposed to be. I whirled around to see if his ghost was floating somewhere in my room. Only I was alone.

"Kip!" I called out. "If you can hear me, just answer one question. Do you want me to help Aileen or Leanna?"

I waited for a reply, but there was none.

Still I sensed his spirit nearby. "Kip, why aren't you showing yourself?"

In my head I had a flash of a light bulb burning out, as if he was trying to tell me his power to crossover was fading.

"You can't leave me like this!" I stomped on the carpet. "Should I go through with my plan to find a new guy for Aileen or Amy's crazy plan to help Leanna?"

When there was no whisper of an answer, I intuitively knew that I'd heard the last from Kip.

From now on, I was on my own.

*   *   *

I was also on my own with schoolwork.

Independent study continued to be a major pain. It was either mind-numbingly boring or too confusing without a teacher to ask for help. I started to long for crowded classrooms, the stench of cafeteria food, and lame comments from teachers. Mostly I longed for my friends.

Before Mom left for some meeting about urban improvements, she looked through my assignments and was quick to voice her disappointment with my progress. "You haven't done your language arts worksheet or the math assignments."

I promised to work harder, but once she was gone I only finished three math problems before my mind shifted to other topics—like a damaged saber, Kip's bloody computer message, and Nona's failing health. Why was I wasting time with schoolwork when I should be solving *real* problems?

So I put my textbooks away and picked up the phone and called Nona. Only Penny-Love answered.

"Hey!" I said, glad to hear her voice. It felt like centuries since we'd talked rather than just a few days. "Ditching school again?"

"I never ditch school," she said with an indignant sniff. "I always have a legitimate excuse from my mother."

"Signed by you."

"Details, details." She giggled. "I had a good reason today. Soul-Mate Matches is swamped and this is the only way to get caught up. My promo idea of a discount flyer in the newspaper made us crazy busy."

"So get back to work and put Nona on."

"Now isn't a good time." There was a pause. "She's busy with a client."

"Tell her to call me when the client leaves. I need some professional advice."

"Problems with Josh?"

"Nothing like that. I have this friend who needs romantic help."

"Ah, a romance SOS! My specialty. Tell me about it."

So I did, and when I finished Penny-Love was all about solutions. "Here's what you're gonna do. I'm going to email you a personal form for Aileen to fill out."

"She won't do it."

"Figure out the information yourself."

"How am I supposed to do that?"

"Be creative," she said with a chuckle. Then she clicked off to get another call.

I stared at the phone for a few minutes, feeling like I'd been manipulated, which was certainly the truth. Penny-Love had pushed my problem back to me without telling me anything about Nona.

After printing out the form for Aileen, I was able to fill in some basic information like her name, address, school, age, and phone number. But that left about a dozen personal questions. Favorite foods, hobbies, music, tattoos?

Be creative, huh?

I considered the creative strategies Manny had used to get interviews for the *Sheridan Shout-Out*. Once he'd dressed up as a pizza delivery guy, heated a frozen pizza and put it in a carton. A few hours later he had his interview, plus a generous tip. Another time he'd posed as a teacher over the phone and faked a parent-teacher conference.

But I'd rather not lie, except as a last resort.

Aileen would still be in school, so I'd call her later. Or even better, I'd surprise her with a visit this evening if Mom, Dad, and my sisters were in the mood for Chinese food. We hadn't eaten together once since I returned, and it was starting to bug me. We could be the poster family for dysfunctional families. Mom's warp-speed schedule was hard to keep up with. And Dad was even worse. I'd seen more of Kip, which was sad considering he was dead. Going out to dinner would be good for us.

With this decided, I returned to my depressing piles of schoolwork.

After a few hours of mounting frustration, I finished the English report and two math assignments. I still had an essay to write on a controversial woman in politics. A search online had gotten me started, but I needed to hit the library for more information.

The library was only a few blocks away, and after consulting Mrs. Sweeny the librarian, I found some great resources. I checked out three books and printed articles from newspaper archives. As I scanned back issues, I ran across a small article about the band Arcadia High had hired for their upcoming prom.

I shivered, knowing the festive prom would result in a funeral.

That's when it occurred to me that this was an opportunity to find out more about Kip's accident. I'd only seen the one article from a small local newspaper. I'd never read any follow-up reports or checked competing papers. On a hunch, I searched back issues and found two more articles. One was short, just a paragraph, but the other covered half a page and included a gruesome photo of twisted metal wreckage next to a cheerful yearbook photo of Kip.

At first I didn't notice anything unusual.

The report included vivid details of the prom; crowning ceremony for the new crowned king and queen, the band that I recognized because Vin raved about them, a list of faculty chaperones including Mr. Landreth, and the colorful balloons raining from the ceiling as the evening finale.

Then the tone switched to graphic gore with quotes from the first officer on the accident scene and an interview with Arcadia High's football coach, who raved about Kip's athletic promise and said losing such a talent had devastated the entire community. The principal praised Kip, bringing back my own painful memories of going to the principal's office and being shown the "Kick Sabine Out of School" petition. Over a hundred signatures, but only one that mattered.

My mind drifted over the rest of the article, until one sentence jumped out at me. Huh? But that wasn't right. I read it again:

The tragic accident occurred at approximately 1:15 a.m., after Kip Hurst dropped off his girlfriend, Aileen Paladini, a senior from Arcadia High, at her residence on Leonora Way.

But the timeline didn't fit with Aileen's story. She said they'd only stayed at the prom a few hours, sneaking out before the royalty crowning ceremony to go to a nearby motel, arguing and never going inside. Then Kip dropped Aileen off at her home "so early the prom was still going on." Which meant the accident would have occurred before midnight—not after one.

So either the newspaper reported the time wrong.

Or Aileen was lying.

23

That night we ate Chinese at Chopsticks Cafe—
and it would have been a perfect evening except
for three things.

1. My father didn't come home from
   work. (No surprise there.)

2. My sisters got into an argument and stopped talking.
3. Aileen wasn't working.

The food at Chopsticks was fabulous, but I was left with a sour taste in my mouth and an overall sense of failure. And I wouldn't get a chance to talk with Aileen for at least two days because tomorrow I'd promised to go with Amy to the Hurst house. Against my better judgement, we were going to conjure up some "black magic."

Heaven help us.

It was a mystery how Amy managed to con Leanna into this wacko plan. But Amy was excited and positive it would work. "Leanna thinks you have magic powers, so she'll believe whatever you tell her," my sister insisted. If it helped Leanna get over her brother's death, I'd give it a try.

Then tomorrow I'd tackle Aileen's love life.

I had gone out in the backyard and collected green leaves and wild grass to pass off as witchy ingredients. I'd found a dark blue bowl and six yellow candles in the kitchen. Not exactly like the spell required, but Leanna was only ten years old—how would she know the difference?

After struggling through another morning of stay-at-homework, Amy and I arrived at the Hurst house.

"Shssh!" Leanna put her finger to her lips when she opened the door for us. "My mother is watching her soaps upstairs." Then she led us into her room.

"Is that the stuff?" Leanna pointed to the paper bag I held after closing her door behind us.

"Yeah." I tried to act serious, but I had the ridiculous urge to laugh. I mean, this whole plan was absurd.

"What do we do first?" Leanna asked. She kept her gaze fixed on me with a mixture of awe and fear. "Will it hurt?"

"Don't be a baby," Amy told her friend. "This is a forgiveness ceremony. You're lucky Sabine said she'd do it. Not many people get to see her powers."

"She really has witch powers?"

"Well, duh." Amy flipped her long dark hair over her shoulder, giving Leanna an annoyed look. "If you don't believe, we'll leave right now."

"I believe. I believe," she said hastily, her eyes wide with fear. "But will getting a spell hurt?"

"Of course not."

Then Amy prepared the spell. She'd taken out the candles, arranged them in a circle on the metal tray, and placed the dark blue bowl at the center. My sister glanced up at me expectantly. "What next, Sabine?"

"Uh . . . crush the chicory and dandelion."

Amy did as I asked, and I thought I heard Opal's laugh in my head. "You think this is funny?" I thought to my spirit guide.

Abundantly amusing. I wouldn't miss it for all the worlds.

"Thanks," I said sarcastically. Then I glanced over at the younger girls and realized I'd spoken out loud. So I covered quickly by saying we needed to meditate and give thanks to the guiding spirits.

You're welcome, Opal told me. *Don't neglect to ask for protective light and invoke blessings from your angels.*

I lifted my hands over the waving smoke from the candles and spoke in a monotone, "I ask for a white light of protection."

And angels, Opal reminded. *Most people don't realize it, but angels can be rather self-important and they crave adoration.*

"And may our angels in all their splendor shine their grace upon us." Is that good enough? I thought to Opal.

Excellent.

I was really getting into this now, and used some of the meditation techniques Nona had taught me. Breathing in and out, opening my mind, and welcoming positive energy.

"Is Kip here?" Leanna asked, gnawing at a thumbnail. She looked nervously around her bedroom.

"Not yet." I shook my head. "To summon him speak his name three times."

"Like that movie *Beetlejuice*?"

I nodded, wondering if that's where I got the idea. Well, no matter.

"Let's say it together," I told Leanna. "Kip . . . Kip . . . Kip."

Our voices echoed in the room, sounding so spooky that shivers rose on my skin. I had no idea if Kip would show up, but I would bet he heard us.

"What now?" Amy asked with an uneasy glance at me. I could tell she wasn't sure how real this was.

I held out the dark blue bowl to Leanna. "Crush the snake root leaf and grass—"

Sabine dear, I don't mean to interrupt, but I should warn you . . .

Leave me alone, Opal. I'm busy right now.

But there's something you should be aware of.

I can handle this without your interference.

Interference is coming anyway.

And just then the door burst open.

My sister Ashley had arrived.

*   *   *

"I knew you guys were up to something," Ashley said, her blue eyes shining black with anger. She folded her arms across her chest and glared at us. "Are you having a party without me?"

"Butt out," Amy snapped at her twin.

"My butt's gonna stay right here until you fess up. Why are you trying to steal my friend?"

Leanna shook her head. "It's not like that."

"Yeah, right," she scoffed. "Amy's always taking my stuff, and now she's after my friends, too."

"Do not!" Amy retorted. "You're the one who takes *my* stuff."

"Whatever." Ashley turned to Leanna and asked in a low, hurt tone. "You told me you had a violin lesson today and I believed you until I was out riding my bike and saw Mom's car out front. At first I thought our moms were visiting, until I remembered Sabine drives that car. Then I find you in here—the room you wouldn't even let me see—with my sisters. Don't you like me anymore?"

Leanna looked close to tears. "I like you a lot."

"Then why the secrets?"

"I—I didn't mean . . . it's hard to explain."

"And what's with the candles?" Ashley squinted down at the bowl and assorted ingredients. Slowly her gaze shifted to me. "And why are *you* here?"

While Amy trusted and believed in my abilities, Ashley was more like Mom and got uncomfortable with any paranormal talk. So I hesitated, not sure how to answer.

"Sabine, are you messing with that weirdness again?"

"Uh . . . define weirdness."

She narrowed her expression into accusation. "Mom is going to be so mad. You promised not to do these things."

"What's she gonna do? Kick me out?"

Leanna looked between us, then said quickly, "I asked Sabine to help me." Then she explained about arguing with Kip before he died and how she never got to apologize, so we were performing a forgiveness ceremony.

I wasn't sure how Ashley would react, but I didn't expect her to burst out laughing—which is exactly what she did.

"What's so funny?" I asked when Ashley paused to catch her breath. "This is a very serious ceremony."

Leanna nodded. "We have a sacred bowl, chicory, and snake root."

"Oh, spare me." Ashley waved her hand in a dismissive gesture. "I collected leaves for a school project and that's not snake root. It's an oak leaf."

"An oak leaf?" Leanna repeated in surprise. "How can Kip forgive me with only an oak leaf?"

"Substitutions work okay," Amy said.

"That bowl is the one we made chocolate chip cookies in last week," Ashley added.

"Those were great cookies." Leanna frowned, narrowing her gaze at Amy. "Is this really the same bowl?"

Amy shrugged. "The bowl doesn't matter."

"All your mumbo-jumbo doesn't matter either," Ashley declared. "There's no such thing as a forgiveness ceremony."

"There isn't?" Leanna's mouth fell open.

"My sisters are tricking you."

"We're trying to help," I insisted.

"By faking witchcraft?" Ashley challenged.

"If it's not real, it won't work." Leanna sank in a chair, as if all hope drained out of her. "Kip will always hate me."

"You really think that?" Ashley asked incredulously. "Just because you had an argument before he died?"

"He said he'd never forgive me."

"So what? My sisters and I argue all the time and say worse things. Amy whines that I'm mean to her—which is so not true—and Sabine ignores me like I'm a baby in diapers."

"I do not!" I argued.

"Ashley's right," Amy said with an apologetic glance at me. "Sometimes you have this superior attitude and brush us off."

"Me brush you off? You're the ones always rushing off to classes and appointments."

"Which you don't consider important," Ashley pointed out. "Like modeling is a childish dress up game."

"I never said that."

"But you thought it," Amy said, softening her words with an apologetic tone. "Whenever I talk about an audition or job, you roll your eyes."

Amy and Ashley gave me identical accusing looks. I was too stunned to argue, and a little ashamed because they might be right. Could I be jealous? Well . . . maybe a little. Not because I wanted what they had, but because everyone fussed over them and seemed to forget I existed. And the only talent I had scared my mother. Still that wasn't my sisters' faults, and I needed to treat them like mature young women. So I swallowed my pride and told them I was sorry.

Amy hugged me, while Ashley smiled triumphantly and turned to Leanna. "See what I mean? We fight a lot and still love each other."

"But Kip hated me when he died and—" Leanna's eyes filled with tears. "And I—I didn't get to say I was sorry."

"I repeat: So what?" Ashley tossed her dark hair over her shoulder and turned to me. "Sabine, let's pretend you and I got into a big fight and you called me a selfish brat. So I yelled back, 'You're the worst sister in the world and I wish you were dead.' Then you choke on a piece of pizza and die. Would you still be mad at me?"

"Of course not." I tried not to smile as I added, "Even if you are a selfish brat, I'd still love you."

"And I wouldn't wish you were dead even though you're bossy." Ashley turned back to Leanna. "Fighting is normal in families. I don't really think Sabine is the worst sister in the world—I'm sure there are lots worse. Sometimes we just say things without thinking. That's what sisters—and brothers, I guess—do."

"Ashley's right," I told Leanna. "Kip isn't mad at you."

"Did his ghost tell you that?"

Before I could answer, Ashley snorted. "Pul—leeze! Why would your brother—even if he was a ghost, which I seriously doubt—talk to my sister instead of his own? You don't need a séance to talk to your brother."

"It wasn't a séance, but Ashley has a point," I said. "You don't need a ceremony to let Kip know how you feel. Just say the words. He will hear you."

"Are you sure?"

"Cross my heart and hope to—"

"Yeah, whatever." Ashley put up her hand to cut me off. "Don't finish that."

I smiled to myself.

Leanna went over to the shrine table and picked up the picture of Kip. Holding it close to her face, she whispered, "I'm sorry."

The lights in the room flickered.

Leanna's eyes widened, then she relaxed into the first genuine smile I'd ever seen from her. I noticed with some satisfaction that Ashley looked spooked. Not quite the skeptic now, I wanted to tell her. But I maturely refrained.

"Mom has been bugging me to let her redecorate and I'm ready now. I don't really need all these pictures and stuff on my walls to remember Kip," Leanna picked up a framed photo from the center of her shrine. "I'll put the others away, and keep this one out."

"I think Kip would like that," I said approvingly.

"Yeah. He would." Leanna glanced around the bedroom as if sensing something that even I couldn't see.

No one spoke for a moment, then Ashley moved toward the door. "Okay, that's done. Let's move on to something fun. Know what we should do?"

"What?" I asked.

Ashley winked at me. "Pizza anyone?"

24

After so much drama, the next morning I was let down.

Mostly I studied and worked on the computer. All very dull, except when the phone rang and I heard Nona's voice full of energy and humor. We brainstormed ways to find a nice guy for Aileen, although it all hinged on convincing Aileen to fill out the Soul-Mate Matches questionnaire. Nona suggested I tell Aileen it's a school project or find a personality quiz in a magazine to give her. Both were good ideas and after we hung up, I tried calling Aileen. Only I got a machine and left a message that wasn't returned.

Was she avoiding me? I wondered.

That evening Dad showed up for dinner.

Great, right? Well it would have been if not for the distinct chilly aura between my parents. I suspected Dad was only there because Mom issued him some kind of ultimatum. "Act like part of this family or get out for good." Whatever she said worked, and I was glad he was here. I'd always been closer to him than with Mom. He was easy-going, relaxed, and affectionate. Not big into discipline, he rarely criticized me, and I loved to laugh at even his corniest lawyer jokes. Sharing a meal together, I could almost pretend we were a happy family.

Unfortunately it didn't last long. After dinner, Dad disappeared into his office, the door firmly shut. Mom watched him leave with this tight, angry expression. Then she told us girls to clean up and stormed off to her bedroom, another shut door.

The tension was thick and uncomfortable, so after helping my sisters with the dishes, I left, too. I'd already planned to work tonight at the fencing center to show everyone there I wasn't a wimp. My cut looked awful—jagged and crusty red—but it didn't hurt. It hurt more to have to dig in my closet for an old pair of fencing pants.

Entering the fencing center, I held my breath, as if expecting something bad to happen—but nothing did. Kevin even brought me a get-well card with a sad-eyed puppy picture with floppy ears and a droopy red tongue on the front. Inside he wrote in large, uneven handwriting, "You're the best teacher. You're an awesome fencer. Love Kevin."

When I hugged him, he turned redder than the sad-eyed puppy's tongue.

The Foils were there, too, except for the new girl Annika. There wasn't any time to talk with them because the beginners kept me busy. Still, during break, my gaze drifted over to their practice session, focusing on Brianne. She fenced with such intensity it was like watching a thrilling dance. She didn't switch off partners, staying with Tony; like a hummingbird paired with a strong ox. Tony's style was more athletic and he grunted and got red in the face, while Brianne achieved more in small, precise moves. But the furious pace wore her down, and on a parry, she jerked back with a cry, folding her arm against her side like a bird's damaged wing. She must have pulled a muscle because she winced when Tony drew her close. She melted against him so snugly, she seemed to vanish in his shadow.

It made me uneasy to watch them together, and I was glad to return to teaching after break. By the time class was over, I was proud of how the students were coming along. I'd had a chance to hone my own skills, too, in a few demonstrations.

"Good form," Mr. Landreth said as we left the floor.

"I'm rusty with fourth position."

"I couldn't tell. You've still got it."

"Well . . . thanks." I felt a rise in confidence as I shook off my canvas jacket.

"Sabine, do you have a minute?" His expression grew serious and he cleared this throat. "Could we talk privately a moment?"

"Sure." I followed him to a quiet corner where we sat on a bench.

"There's something I'd like to ask you, and hear me out before refusing."

"Go ahead," I said with caution. "What's up?"

"You may have noticed that Annika was missing."

I nodded. "Is she sick?"

"No. Her aunt died."

"Oh, that's too bad." I remembered the auburn-haired girl's sad expression and how Jennae put her arm around her last night. Now I understood. "I'm sorry."

"So am I." He sighed. "There was a long illness and the family knew it was coming soon. The funeral is being held this Saturday in Pennsylvania."

He didn't say anything for a few moments, letting this sink in. Of course I knew what he was going to ask. This Saturday was the Renaissance Festival. And now the Foils were missing a fencer.

My heart sped up. A chance to turn back time, to perform again, to be part of this group I'd once loved so much. Wearing the jacket embroidered with the silver Foils emblem and the matching silver fencing pants. Being admired, hearing cheers, belonging.

"No," I said firmly.

"We could really use you."

"It shouldn't be hard to find someone else."

"There is no one else."

"I just can't." I shook my head.

"It would just be this once." He spread out his hands imploringly. "Please, Sabine. We need you."

I shook my head. "Sorry."

Then I grabbed my bag and fled.

* * *

That night I talked for over an hour on the phone to Josh. I told him about independent study and shared some cheerleading gossip that Penny-Love had passed on. My words were ripples across a calm lake; surface only without sinking into deep territory. I didn't mention fencing, ghosts, or how it was Dominic I thought of when Josh said he missed me.

"I miss you, too," I said, determined to make it true.

As I drifted off to sleep that night, I was feeling more in control of my life.

The next afternoon, after struggling with home studies, I tried Aileen's number one more time—and she answered. Stunned, I hardly knew what to say and asked if I could see her. Not only did she invite me over, but she sounded eager to see me.

And when she answered the door a short while later, she was grinning with excitement. But it turns out she was more excited about seeing my car.

"Don't put away your keys," she told me in a rush. "I was wishing for a way to go out and here you are." She shut the front door behind her. "I have to take the bus or get my parents to drive me places. But my folks are working and I'm stuck here with no wheels. Will you give me a ride?"

"Sure." I shrugged. "Where to?"

"On a mission of mercy," she said dramatically, bouncing into the passenger seat of my car in her bunny-nervous mode. "On a fast food run. I am totally craving a double cheeseburger with extra sauce and onion rings."

I laughed. Aileen didn't look like she was a fast food junkie. She must have a fast metabolism to stay so petite. I'd only had soup for lunch and could go for a strawberry shake and fries. Bonding over food would be a good way to squeeze info out of Aileen.

While she placed our order, I sat in a booth, glancing down at the magazine I'd brought along. I was going with Nona's idea of a quiz and borrowed the latest *High Fives* Magazine, which had a great self-awareness quiz. My plan was to pull it out while we were deep in fried food and carbs, and adding some of my own questions to the magazine's quiz.

Then if I got a chance, I'd also find out what time Kip's accident occurred. Before or after midnight? The time discrepancy bothered me, like an itch I couldn't reach. But I couldn't just blurt out such a sensitive question. So I'd start with the easy ones.

Aileen rolled her eyes when she saw the magazine. "That's so junior high. Aren't you too old for that?"

I dipped a fry into ketchup and leaned back in the orange plastic booth. "This belongs to my sister. I was bored and started doing the quiz. You ever do quizzes?"

"No." She picked up her double cheeseburger with both hands and took a bite.

"Hey, it could be fun," I persisted. "Like how would you answer this question: If you won the lottery, what would you buy first? A) A hot car B) New clothes C) Electronic Games D) Nothing. You'd put it in the bank."

I crossed my fingers under the table and hoped she'd play along.

She finished chewing and shrugged. "Easy."

"A car?" I guessed.

"No way. Gas is too expensive and I can't afford insurance on my wages. But I got my eye on the latest version of Demonic Dragons, so my answer would be C. I love games."

"Really?" I wouldn't have guessed that, and made a mental note. Since I had her attention, I went to the next question. "What kind of movie do you prefer? A) Horror B) Adventure C) Romance D) Forget the movies, I'd rather read a good book."

She chose B.

And she'd rather vacation at the ocean than a theme park, receive a gift of flowers instead of expensive jewelry, and she liked tropical fish for pets. I shared some of my answers, too, so she wouldn't be suspicious, and we were still talking after our food was gone.

Aileen confided that she was into role-playing games and part of an online D&D group. "Only we lost our DM," she added with a sigh. "Turns out he was only nine and his parents took away his computer as a punishment for not eating broccoli. Isn't that barbaric? Now we're minus a player."

"Too bad. Is it hard to find a new dungeon master?"

"Yeah. We don't want just anyone, but the best. We take the rules seriously and don't allow cheating. We need someone who's honest and knowledgeable."

"And over nine," I joked.

"That would help. Know anyone?"

I pondered my scribbled answers on the quiz. I had enough information about Aileen to fill out her Soul-Mates form and find a guy so perfect she wouldn't be able to resist going out with him. But something jabbed my memory. Fast food and D&D gaming—why did that combo sound so familiar?

Then the pieces clicked together. I could almost hear Opal laughing at me, saying it took me long enough to find the right solution.

"Aileen," I said excitedly. "I *do* know someone."

Her face lit up. "A good D&D player?"

"The best! He even keeps a handbook in his car."

"So he drives?" She grinned. "Then he must be over nine."

"Definitely."

And I gave her Alphonso's number.

*　　*　　*

On the drive back to Aileen house's, I was feeling really good about matching her up with Alphonso. They weren't the types you'd expect to pair up; she was petite and more the bubbly cheerleader type while everything about him shouted "Geek!" Playing D&D wasn't a romantic date, but it was a start. I knew in my soul that they would be good for each other. He'd treat her with the respect she deserved and she was talkative enough for both of them. Once they bonded over fast food and D&D, anything could happen. And I was counting on it.

But I couldn't leave Aileen without asking one more question. So when we reached her house, I glanced over at her.

"Can I ask you something about Kip?" I spoke carefully.

"Sure," she replied with easy trust. "What?"

"I was at the library a few days ago, going through old newspapers for a report, and I came across an article about the car crash." Clicking my seatbelt off, I shifted toward her. "Only the timing didn't fit. They said he crashed *after* one in the morning."

"No way," Aileen said with a shake of her dark head. "Kip dropped me off around eleven."

"That's what I thought."

"The reporter got it wrong or it's a typo."

"Yeah. That must be it," I said, relieved that it was something so innocent.

"I got home before the prom was even over. Kip drove off so fast . . ." Her gaze drifted out the window. "I was in bad shape for a while and didn't read or watch any news."

"But the police must have interviewed you?"

"Oh, they showed up, but my parents talked for me. I was either crying or sleeping and not making any sense. My parents probably told them I got home after the prom, since I was too upset to talk to anyone and came in the back door. That could be why the timing is off."

"But wouldn't the police know the time of the accident?"

"You'd think," she said with a shrug.

"Yet the newspaper reported Kip crashed at 1:15. Could he have gone somewhere else after he dropped you off?"

"Where? All our friends were still at the prom." She seemed flustered, reaching down to open her purse. She pulled out a wallet and flipped open to some pictures.

I looked down at small photos from the prom. "We had these pictures taken . . . just hours before . . ." Her voice cracked. "See how happy we were? Smiling like nothing bad could ever happen."

Her sadness reached out like ghostly fingers tightening around me. I could hardly breathe and fought to stay in control by focusing on the photo. The happy couple; Aileen lovely in a lavender chiffon sleeveless dress, and Kip was grinning down at her. He wore jeans with a formal jacket and looked really hot, with dimples and deep-set eyes and dark wavy hair. I'd heard many hearts were broken when he'd gotten serious with Aileen. But some girls don't consider guys hands-off even when they're in a serious relationship. There were even football groupies who made a game of scoring with players.

After Aileen said no, had Kip found a yes with someone else?

There were more photos from prom night, several of couples I didn't know and a group shot of football players with their dates. I gave a little gasp when I saw Tony and Brianne, although it shouldn't have been a surprise. I'd helped her decide on the ruby red dress and experiment with different hairstyles until she'd settled on an upswept style with ringlets sweeping down her cheeks. If things had been different, Brianne and I would have hung together after the prom and giggled over who-did-what-with-whom. But that night changed everything.

The photos blurred and dizziness slammed into me. I reached for something to hold onto, only my hands slipped through air. I was jerked backwards, tumbling out of my own body, sinking into a dark void.

When I could see clearly, I wasn't in my car anymore—instead I was with Kip on prom night.

He was solid flesh, and I was the ghost. We rode together on a dark road, through inky night, lit only by the whirl of passing streetlights. The road zoomed by as Kip increased his speed.

He pulsed with fiery anger, driving with such fury that I suspected he was either being chased or doing the chasing. His knuckles on the steering wheel pale as death and an eerie glow from the car's dash reflected crazed purpose in his eyes.

My view shifted and I focused in on the illuminated numbers on the dash. 1:09. So the newspaper was right. But what had happened during that missing time? His passenger seat was empty except for a piece of red silky ribbon and crushed rose petals spilled like crimson drops of blood.

Ribbon and petals from a corsage.

I snapped to reality, back with Aileen in my own car.

My jaw dropped as I stared at Aileen, then down at the photos she still held in her slender fingers. She'd worn a lavender gown with a purple corsage. Not red with silk ribbon and roses, but lilacs.

Only one girl in the group photo wore red. My heart tightened and it was hard to keep from gasping. She stood on the other side of Kip, her gaze not on her own date, but smiling up adoringly at Kip. A lovely corsage with roses as bright as crimson flame was pinned to her flowing ruby gown.

Brianne.

25

It took more courage than I possessed to call Brianne, yet I did anyway. Only her mother, who used to say she loved me like her second daughter, lied and told me Brianne wasn't home. She had the decency to say she was sorry, which she deserved to be. In the background, I heard Brianne's low voice.

She wouldn't talk to me and now I knew why. Not because we weren't friends anymore, but because we'd been so very close; sister-friends who built imaginary kingdoms and shared secrets at sleepovers. She knew about my ghosts and feared them—feared what they would tell me. She was afraid I'd see her truth; the secret she'd tried so hard to hide.

I knew she'd been at the prom, although I never connected her to Kip. If I hadn't been so hurt by losing her friendship, I might have thought more clearly and realized it would take something huge for her to turn against me.

Like death.

While Brianne didn't see ghosts, she knew I did. I'd amazed her many times by knowing things without being told. If she had a guilty conscience, I was the last person she'd want around. Is that why she signed the petition? To force me out of her life to guard her secret?

As I laid in bed that night, tossing aside my covers and unable to sleep, I took scraps of facts like quilt fragments and pieced them together. Brianne had gone to the prom with Tony, but she wasn't serious about him. In fact, she'd hinted there was another jock she liked. Was it Kip? She liked a challenge, and what was more challenging than going after a hot guy who already had a girl-friend?

Aileen and Kip left the dance early, but if the newspaper account was true, there was over two hours of unaccounted time. I flashed on the image of rose petals and red silky ribbon. Ripped, crushed, lifeless.

How had petals from Brianne's corsage ended up in Kip's car? What had happened between the time Kip dropped Aileen off and the accident?

Brianne would know. I fell asleep with a heavy heart and a sense of dread for what I had to do.

*   *   *

The next morning a strange car drove up to the house and a uniformed guy got out carrying a square silver-wrapped package.

"Delivery for Ms. Sabine Rose," he said, smiling cheerfully when I answered the door.

"I'm Sabine," I said with surprise

"Sign here, please?"

Curious, I signed then fished into my pocket and gave him a tip. The foil wrapped present was smooth to touch as I held it gently in my hands.

Who could it be from? I wondered, setting it on the living room couch. It's not my birthday and too early for Christmas. The wrapping was professional quality, with a glittery gold bow and curling silver-gold blended ribbon.

Untying the ribbon and slicing open the tape with my thumbnail, I ripped off the wrapping. Inside the box I found a ceramic night-light in the shape of a large brown dog. Only close friends knew about my night-light collection. Intrigued, I dug around in the box until I found a small silver card and read:

Sabine,

Hope you like this night-light. Doesn't it remind you of Horse? Think of me when you use it. I wish I could see you this weekend, but Arturo needs me. I miss you.

Love, Josh

Arturo needs me! I thought, tempted to fling the box across the room.

I wasn't fooled for one moment. This wasn't a gift; it was a bribe. Josh's way of saying, "Here's a pretty trinket so you won't be angry that I'm ditching you again." What kind of an idiot did Josh take me for? If he really missed me, he'd show up.

"Damn him!" I fumed, closing the lid on the box and tossing it aside.

Another romantic weekend was ruined. We wouldn't have a chance to reconnect and act like the happy couple we were supposed to be. He loved me! He missed me! Well he had a terrible way of showing it. I'd been trying so hard to figure out my feelings for him, to banish all thoughts of Dominic and create a perfect relationship with Josh, but I couldn't do it alone.

Why were Arturo's needs more important than mine? You'd think Amazing Arturo had real powers of magic, instead of stage tricks. He'd turned my reliable, sweet boyfriend into an irresponsible jerk.

I was tempted to call Josh and let him know exactly what I thought of his precious Arturo. But if I complained, I'd only come off pathetic and whiny. And I didn't want to be one of those needy girls who hung on their boyfriends like a noose.

"I don't need any guy to define me," I told myself as I picked up the gift and carried it into my bedroom. "I have plenty of friends and even a job with a boss who respects me."

Impulsively I picked up the phone and called Mr. Landreth. He literally whooped for joy when I told him I'd changed my mind, that I would be happy to replace Annika after all.

"Take that, Josh," I said, stabbing the air with the phone as if it were a sword and I'd just skewered my so-not devoted boyfriend.

Then I ripped his card into confetti.

*　　*　　*

Josh didn't call. And I refused to care.

I burned up phone lines talking to Penny-Love, Manny, Thorn, and Vin. My ear was still ringing from Vin's excitement when I told him I was temporarily returning to Foils. He was sure I'd want to stay permanently and suggested I replace Annika. "I'm sorry about her aunt, but truth is she's not half as good as you. She only got in the group 'cause she was dating Derrick."

"Annika and Derrick? I didn't know they were together."

"They aren't any more," Vin explained. "It only lasted a few weeks and they're just friends now. Annika is back with some guy from her last school, and Derrick is looking. You know how relationships revolve in Foils." He went on about his own sadly lacking love life then segued into news about people I'd used to know when I went to Arcadia High. I enjoyed listening and curled into an oversized pillow on my bed, glancing over at a dresser with fencing trophies.

The next day, I woke up with serious second thoughts.

Performing with Foils again? What had I been thinking?

Call it stage fright or a reality check, but I felt a rush of panic and wished I'd never agreed to fill in for Annika. I hadn't even practiced with them. My skills were rusty and I wasn't even sure my uniform fit. It probably smelled musty too, locked away in a bottom drawer for half a year. I had to call Mr. Landreth right away and tell him I couldn't go through with the exhibition.

Maybe I would have.

But I'll never know because after I got dressed and was brushing my hair, there was a commotion from downstairs, knocking, and then a thump of footsteps.

Then I heard someone call my name, so I went out in the hall and saw—

"Ohmygod!" I squealed, not quite believing my eyes. "Thorn! Manny!"

My Goth friend arched the silver stud in her brow and combed her black-pearl polished fingernails through her plastic-looking black-and-mauve wig. Beside her, Manny's black dreads were beaded like rattling snakes and wiggled around his dark, grinning face. He wrapped me in a warm hug.

"Looking good, Sabine. Surprised to see us?"

"Thrilled. What are you doing here?"

"I'm wondering that, too," Thorn said in a dry tone. I could tell she was glad to see me, but she would rather die than show emotion. She wore a pleated black skirt that trailed in an uneven hem along the carpet and black lace over a hot pink T-shirt with metal chains.

"So what's for breakfast?" Manny asked with a glance toward the kitchen. "We left at an ungodly hour to get here and haven't eaten. How about eggs benedict with whipped creamed waffles?"

"I wish!" I chuckled, feeling ridiculously happy. Having them here was like having a piece of my other life back, making me ache even more to move back to Sheridan Valley.

Over plain toast and cereal, I learned it was Thorn's idea to drive here for the Renaissance Fair.

"Not to see me?" I asked teasingly.

"That too." She shrugged. "I go to these fairs with my friends a lot to check out reproductions of swords and chains."

"Weapons don't interest me, but I like all the ye old English talk and costumes, especially the fair wenches in tight-laced bodices," Manny added with a wicked grin.

Thorn smacked him on the arm, but he didn't notice.

Having them with me eased my nervousness and gave me a boost of confidence. When I told them I would be performing with Foils, they were impressed and promised to clap louder than any other spectators.

We climbed in Thorn's yellow jeep. I wore jeans and a sweatshirt, carrying my equipment bag and planning to switch into my Foil's costume later. After parking about a mile away, we walked along a narrow dirt path to the fair and were passing through the entrance where festive flags and banners snapped in a brisk breeze. Up ahead, I caught a flash of a silver fencing shirt with the Foils emblem. For a moment I thought it was Brianne and this would be my chance to talk to her. But the girl was taller, with reddish hair, and I recognized Jennae.

"Mr. L. told me you didn't want to come today," she said, studying me with an odd expression.

"That's true," I admitted. "I've been away for so long, and don't want to embarrass the group."

"You could never do that, you're too good a fencer." The way she said "too good" didn't sound like a compliment, but more of a complaint.

"Well, thanks. I love fencing."

"So much that you'd do anything to get back in the group?" she accused. "Even if it meant kicking someone else off the team?"

The hostility in her voice shocked me. "What are you getting at?"

"Vin was going around saying you were going to take Annika's place."

"He *what*?"

"Sure she's not that good yet, but she's really trying. She almost didn't go to her aunt's funeral because she was afraid she'd lose her place in the group."

So that's why Jennae had been acting weird toward me—she was protecting her friend. I assured her that I would never take Annika's place. This caused a huge change in her attitude towards me, and she burst into a smile, then wrapped her arms around me in a warm hug.

"I knew you wouldn't do anything so mean!" she exclaimed, then she hurried off to meet some friends.

My friends were waiting, too, and I rejoined them.

Manny spotted a kissing booth with ample-chested wenches in low-cut dresses, and he was off. Thorn groaned while I just laughed.

The Renaissance Fair was held partly outdoors in a grassy park with shady oaks and pines, and also included vendors hawking their goods in a large building. Manny wore a smile on his lipstick-smeared mouth as Thorn dragged us through aisles. The theme from *Titanic* played in a lilting flute melody as we went up and down rows of booths. There were vendors selling stone and crystal jewelry, Celtic and Scottish books, porcelain tea sets, Welsh recipes, Heraldry (history of family crests), decorative wands, airbrush tattoos, and ribbon wreaths that many of the girls wore like halos atop their flowing hair. I stopped to admire the hair wreaths, thinking these might be a cute gift for my sisters, but Thorn dragged me over to a display of weapons.

"Wicked swords!" Manny exclaimed, reaching up to touch a Scottish Basket Hilt Claymore. "But check out the price—$235! For that it better be the real thing."

"If it was real, you'd have to add a few zeros," Thorn retorted.

Instead of sticking out with her dramatic Goth look, Thorn fit in. Chains, black clothes, and wigs were the norm at this fair. She moved slowly down the aisle, studying each of the upright weapons with a rapt expression.

I didn't know much about historical weapons and found it fascinating. There were Victorian-styled swords, an English Civil War Basket Sword, a sword with a skull grinning from the hilt, a four-bladed ax, and an awesome sword called "Witch King" that cost over $300.

There were more reasonably priced weapons, and after much deliberation, Thorn decided on a small curved dagger with a dragon's body and gleaming red glass eyes for only $40. Manny bought a rope necklace with a bulky green stone. And I went back to the booth to buy a pink wreath for Ashley and a blue one for Amy. Impulsively, I purchased a lavender one for myself.

While all of this was fun, I had obligations, too. So we made a stop by the archery area where I dropped off my equipment bag and checked the schedule for the Foil's performance. Not until two o'clock. That left plenty of time to see the fair.

We watched minstrels perform, a fire-breathing demonstration, jugglers, and an archery contest. White canvas tents covered outdoor booths and strolling performers in authentic clothes had loud discussions in Old English. It was surreal and loads of fun.

For lunch we ate meat pies, "ale" (lemonade) from a pewter mug, and fresh scones with strawberry cream. Manny even tasted haggis, which sounded worse than it looked.

A woman walked by carrying a tiny poodle wearing a cloth unicorn horn wrapped around its head. Manny joked that it was a new breed of dog. "A Uni-oodle."

"A poodle-corn," Thorn suggested.

"How about uni-poo?" I added.

Manny wrinkled his nose. "Sounds like something you don't want to step in."

Thorn groaned and rolled her kohl-painted eyes.

A herald came around, blowing a horn and announcing a joust. We all agreed this sounded cool, so went over to the arena and climbed up to the top of the bleachers for a good view of the show. A large man with a plumed hat and layers of period clothing stood on a pedestal and bellowed into a microphone, "Ladies and Gentleman, are we ready to see a joust?"

The bleachers rocked with foot stomping and shouts of "Aye!"

Belgium and draft horses draped in elaborate blankets and wearing suits of armor galloped onto the grassy field. The favorite jouster seemed to be a rider nicknamed "Sir Shiny Guy" and the crowd roared with applause as he waved.

The announcer explained the point system: one point for touch, three points for a broken tip, and four for a shattered tip. "The horses weigh approximately 1500 pounds and carry about 300 pounds of men and armor. And at impact they're moving at twenty-five miles per hour," the announcer added. "These knights put their health and lives on the line for your entertainment."

The crowd stomped and cheered and shouted, "We want blood!"

Thorn was joining in this bloody chant while Manny was staring at a shapely woman selling refreshments in such a tight bodice that if her laces popped, someone could get hurt.

My gaze drifted around the audience, a rowdy bunch of spectators in jeans and T-shirts mixed with others in medieval costumes. One little girl was dressed with fairy wings, an entire family wore royal velvet and crowns, while a costumed dragon posed for pictures.

There was a squawk and I glanced down near the bottom of the bleachers. A large reddish brown bird fluttered to perch on the arm of a guy in a brown period cap, leather breeches, shiny boots, and a loose-sleeved linen tunic. The guy turned, tipping his cap and staring directly at me.

I covered my gasp.

It was Dominic.

26

I'm not sure what I said, but I was up and pushing my way through crowded bleachers. A chubby man wearing a green frog hat and holding a foaming beer blocked my way, and I had to climb down into the next row, cut over to an aisle, then hurry down the steps. Behind me I heard Manny's voice, but I ignored it. I'd explain later—after I caught up with Dominic.

What was he doing here anyway? His clothes were those of a Renaissance peasant, and for all I knew he might be a regular at Renaissance Fairs. Or was he here to see me? This thought made my heart jump, and I realized that I was happy to see him. More than happy—I wanted to be *with* him. How was that possible? Was I on the rebound? Maybe because Josh stood me up twice and our only contact lately was on the phone or email. I was starting to forget what it was like to be together.

But it was more than that. I didn't really care that Josh wasn't here, not the way I found myself caring about Dominic, wanting to know if he felt anything for me. Maybe it was time to find out . . .

The announcer was shouting something about showing support for the jousters, and suddenly everyone in the bleachers stood up and chanted, "Knock him off! Knock him off!" I was swallowed in a sea of shouts and bodies, and by the time everyone sat down, Dominic was nowhere in sight.

Frustrated but not defeated, I left the arena and continued my search. The smart thing would have been to go back and ask Thorn, who had a psychic talent for finding things (and occasionally people), to help. But this didn't occur to me until I was far from the arena and near a recreated village of canvas tents. But it was eerie and silent, empty of people since everyone was still cheering on the jousters. I walked to the remote Games of Sport area that was enclosed by a wooden rail fence, arranged with piles of haystacks and a display of historical weaponry; arrows, swords, knives, and staffs. Nearby a tent for changing clothes and stowing equipment billowed as a breeze sailed through the partly open flap. Inside, I saw a silver flash of movement.

The flap opened and out stepped Brianne.

She wore her Foil's uniform and carried a cloth bag. When she noticed me, she dropped the bag, and it fell silently to the soft, grassy ground.

"What are you doing here?" she demanded.

"I was looking for a friend . . . but I found you instead."

Her cheeks flamed and as she caught the implication of my words. She looked around the way a wild animal does when it's trapped. "I—I have things to do, so if you'll excuse me," she said.

"No," I spoke firmly. "I won't excuse you because what you did was horrible, and don't you dare walk away."

"You can't make me talk to you," she snapped.

"Would you rather I talk to the police?"

Her skin blanched and a look of fear flickered in her eyes. "I have no idea what you're talking about."

But she did know, and I wasn't letting her off so easily. I'm not sure why it was so important to me to find out what really happened the night Kip died, maybe because Brianne made it personal. Our friendship had died that night, too.

"I don't think you want anyone overhearing this," I told her in a low, determined tone. "Let's go inside the tent."

She opened her mouth to protest, then looked closely at me. Her shoulders sagged, and she nodded, then followed me. I pushed aside the tent flaps and sat on a plastic chair beside Brianne. Being together like this in a private place made me think of all the sleepovers and wonderful secrets we shared in my tree house. This would be the last secret I ever asked of Brianne.

"You were with Kip the night he died," I accused, my voice flat and without question.

"Did you see that in a vision?" she asked sarcastically. "Or was it your spirit guide who told you? How is old Opal these days?"

"It doesn't matter. I just want to know exactly what happened." *And how you could abandon our friendship,* I almost added.

"I'm not telling you anything."

"You'd rather I go straight to the police? They'd be interested to know you're a witness to Kip's death."

"You wouldn't!"

"I will unless you talk." I folded my arms. "Now."

"Fine!" she snapped ungraciously. "But you better not repeat this. Promise?"

"Why should I promise? I already know Kip went back to the prom for you."

"He didn't come back, he called me on my cell phone and I met him."

"So you planned this all along?" I asked with a heavy heart.

Her eyes flashed. "Of course not! Sure, I'd noticed him around and maybe flirted a little, but it was just a kick. It was like a game, sneaking him my phone number and whispering that we should get together later. I didn't expect him to actually call. I mean, he was so crazy about his preppy girl-friend."

"Her name is Aileen."

"Whatever." Brianne scowled. "She could have had him, but she led him on like a tease. He was upset when he called me. All we were going to do was talk."

I didn't believe this, but I allowed her the lie.

"So you ditched your date and went off with Kip. What happened after that?"

"Nothing."

"Then why didn't you tell the police you were with him? Why keep it a secret? Unless his death wasn't an accident."

"It was! A terrible, awful accident! If only he hadn't . . ."

"Hadn't what?"

She shook her head. "Please don't ask. I can't tell you or anyone."

There was an odd fearful note in her voice, and she was glancing around as if expecting some-thing dark and dangerous to appear from a shadowy corner. This wasn't the brave Brianne I remembered.

"Tell me," I insisted, leaning forward and grabbing her arm. She flinched and her sleeve pushed back to reveal dark marks on her arm. Deep purple bruises.

"Ohmygod, Brianne! Who did that to you?"

"He didn't mean to." She jumped to her feet and glared at me. "You can't tell anyone. I mean it, because if you do, he'll get mad and you couldn't handle that."

All the breath oozed out of me as I stared at her. "Tony? He hurts you?"

"It doesn't really hurt," she said hugging her thin arms to her chest. "He's just like that, you know, kind of a hothead."

"He beats you!"

"He gets mad and forgets himself, but he's always sorry."

"And you put up with it?" I just could not believe this.

"He loves me so much that he's afraid of losing me. That's why he came after me that night. He followed me from the prom and found me with Kip. He jerked open the door and yanked me out of Kip's car and started hitting . . ." She shuddered. "I kind of blacked out, I guess."

I was too horrified to speak. Tony had been beating Brianne? And she allowed it? I couldn't fathom this, and felt like I'd fallen in an alternate universe. Brianne was the brave one, the knight rescuing the princess.

"I wasn't out long and when things cleared I knew I was in Tony's car," she went on in a shaky voice. "He was going so fast and I was afraid what he'd do when we stopped. I guess Kip worried about that, too, cause he was chasing us. And getting closer and closer. Tony was swearing and I was afraid he was going to hit me again . . . then I heard the most awful sound in the world." She covered her ears, shuddering. "I still hear it in my dreams . . . a crash so loud and powerful it rocked everything. And when I looked in the back window, there were flames and . . ."

"So he died trying to rescue you?" I asked in an awed breath.

She nodded, trembling.

"And instead of telling anyone, you stayed with Tony?"

"I had to!" she shouted. "Don't you see? They would have blamed me like they blamed you. I knew your predictions were real. Maybe that's why I wanted to be with Tony, to challenge death and prove that I'm stronger than you. But you were right . . . and he died. Then Tony warned me not to say anything. He said they'd arrest us both and he'd be kicked out of sports and everyone would hate me."

"Instead they hated me," I said grimly.

"I'm so sorry." She reached for me, but I backed away. "Sabine, I didn't want to sign that petition. But when I refused, he hit me. I was so stunned, I just did what he wanted. I should have left him . . . yet I was afraid. It was easier to stay, to do what he wanted, and when he's not angry, he can be really sweet. It's not so bad . . ."

"NOT BAD!" I was the one shaking, not with fear, but with outrage. "He's a monster! And you're a fool to let him hit you. If you don't tell someone what he's doing, I'm going to."

"No, you can't," she begged.

"If I don't it'll get worse. I read about guys like him and he won't change. He could end up killing you."

"But he loves me," she whispered sadly. "I can't stop you from talking, but if our friendship ever mattered to you, at least wait until the exhibition is over to tell anyone. Please, Sabine!"

When I wouldn't answer, she seemed to crumple. With a sob, she jumped up and ran through the tent flaps.

I sat there a few moments before getting up, too. But as I stepped outside, I saw Tony coming my way.

"Where's Brianne?" he asked in this chummy nice-guy tone that made my skin crawl."

I shook my head, not meeting his gaze. "Don't know."

"But she's supposed to be here. I told her to wait here for me."

"Well, she's not here."

"So where is she? Did she say anything to you?"

"Brianne and I don't talk much these days," I said with a shrug. My heart was hammering so fast I was sure he could hear it.

"That's too bad about you and Brianne," he said with a sympathetic look. "You used to be really close. Maybe I could talk to Brianne and patch things up between you."

"Don't bother," I said in a tone sharper than I intended.

"What do you mean by that?" He was studying me now, suspicion creeping into his aura. "Are you sure you haven't seen her?"

"No. I haven't."

"She didn't tell you anything?"

"Nothing. I—I have to go." Pushing past him, my fast walk became a run. I was just passing the row of weapons when I felt a firm grip on my wrist and I was thrown to the ground.

Tony, no longer hiding behind a fake smile, glared down at me. "What did that bitch tell you?" he demanded.

"Nothing."

"You're lying."

"Nothing I'd tell you."

I started to get up, but he pushed me back to the ground.

"You asshole! Don't you ever touch me again. I won't put up with it like—"

"Like who?" He leaned closer. "She told you, didn't she?"

"No!" I looked around for help, but I didn't see anyone close by.

"Stay away from Brianne," he threatened. "She'll only tell you lies anyway."

"Lies like her boyfriend hits her?"

"I knew it! What else did she tell you?"

"Nothing!"

He kicked me in the side and I doubled in pain. He stood there, laughing.

"I won't be quiet like her!" From the ground I glared at him.

"Say one word to anyone and you're dead," he threatened. "Want a sample?"

Then before I realized what he planned, he'd reached for one of the Claymore swords in the rack. The sharpened blade flashed like silver death as he waved it toward me.

I jumped to my feet and backed away from him. "Tony, don't do anything dumb."

"Like let you go and open your big mouth?" he said in a growl. "Accidents happen all the time. Like that little boy picking up the wrong sword."

"Did you switch it?" I demanded, looking around for help. But we were in a remote area of the fair and I could still hear distant cheers from the jousting arena.

"What do you think?" There was a crazed look on his face and he lifted the sword. "Ready. Fence."

He swung forward and I jumped sideways. He really was trying to kill me! This was insane!

While he lifted his sword again, I flung myself sideways and grabbed for the rack of weapons. I waved a cutlass at him. "Stay away, Tony!" I shouted.

He laughed again, then in one swing from his side sword he knocked the cutlass from my hands. I grabbed a wooden shield just as his sword came down again. There was a clunk sound as metal slammed into wood. And Tony swore, his anger growing to a frenzy.

He was taller and stronger than me. I could out-fence him in organized fencing, but he was waving a killing weapon and all I had was a chunk of wood. If only I could grab one of the rapiers or axes, then I'd have a chance. But he blocked my way to the rack of weapons.

Don't allow fear to cloud your sensibilities, Opal's voice rang in my ears.

"Help me!" I told her. "Get someone!"

*I'm unable to communicate with others, as you
well know. I would suggest lowering your head . . .
right now.*

I ducked. Swoosh! Tony sword sliced above
my shoulder. I heard him swear and saw that his
swing was so hard, he lost control of the weapon
and it sailed over a haystack, landing out of his
reach. I was a better fencer than he was. If I could
get the sword, he wouldn't have a chance against
me. I could cut him down until he couldn't come
after me again.

But as I scrambled after the fallen weapon, I
heard Opal shout in my head, *No! Abandon your
anger and pay heed to your common sense. Naught
ever comes of violence. Leave the weapon of war and
go forth in defense.*

As confusing as that sounded, I must be getting used to Opal's riddles. Because I knew exactly
what she meant. And in that split second of deci-
sion, instead of going for the weapon and fighting
until blood spilled, I lifted my wooden shield and
flung it with all my strength at Tony.

I heard him cry out, but I didn't stick around.

I took off running and didn't stop screaming
until I found help.

27

The police showed up and had plenty of questions, but Brianne told me to go fence for Foils and offered to talk with them first. All the fight was out of her. I think she just wanted it over.

So a much smaller group of Foil's gave the fencing demonstration. Despite my shaky efforts, it was a good show. At least that's what Manny and Thorn told me afterwards while we were waiting at the police station. They'd come for support, which I really appreciated. I hadn't seen Dominic, and had begun to think I'd imagined him—until I was putting my equipment away and found a note tucked into my bag.

Sabine,

    Sorry I didn't watch you fence. I know you did great—you're really good at everything. I admire that and think about you a lot.

    I'm going after the fourth charm. Could take a few days or a week . . .

    Keep watch on Nona—she's not doing well.

It was simply signed "D."

I stared at the note, rereading his "I admire that and think about you a lot," wondering what he meant by it. Did he care about me the way I suspected I cared about him? If there really was something between us, I couldn't ignore it anymore. Josh was flaking out on me anyway, so maybe it was time to end things. But I'd have to wait for Dominic to return to find out his feelings.

Until then I'd put my heart on hold.

My romantic life might be a mess and Nona was getting worse, but at least I'd done what Kip wanted. I still wasn't sure which girl he'd asked me to help—Leanna, Aileen, or Brianne—but I'd done my best to help them all.

And maybe that's what Kip wanted all along.

*　　*　　*

I'd like to say that my forcing Brianne to tell the truth led to our becoming close friends again. Only that didn't happen.

After the competition we were hustled off to the police station, and she wouldn't even look at me. Maybe she felt I'd betrayed her, and I was okay with that, knowing her bruises, inside and out, would take a long time to heal.

I was still kind of numbed by everything to take it all in. I was also completely exhausted from fighting Tony and answering a barrage of questions. Because I was a minor, I needed a parent present and I chose Dad. He was a lawyer, after all, and I could count on him not to overreact like Mom.

When he arrived at the police station, he showed concern but remained calm and he treated me like an adult, asking questions until he was sure he understood the situation. The police weren't as interested in me once they found out Tony's role in Kip's death and saw Brianne's bruises.

Dad slipped his arm around me and led me to his car.

"You okay?" Dad asked gently as he started up the engine.

"Yeah. Thanks for coming."

"Hey, you're my special girl. I'm always here for you."

"Not lately," I said before I could stop myself. I didn't mean to dredge out bitter feelings now, not after he just helped me.

But he didn't take offense; he reached over to squeeze my hand. "I'm sorry honey. It's not you. It's me."

"And Mom?" I questioned.

He glanced in the rearview mirror, then over at me. "Yes. We're having some problems, but we'll get through this. No worries, okay?"

I smiled at him, and nodded. Being with my father made me feel like a little girl again—safe and protected. But then I thought how he was seldom home and Mom and the girls had such full schedules. Independent study was harder than I expected, and lonely. I wanted to go home . . . with Nona.

Before I lost my courage, I explained to Dad how I felt and asked if I could move back. "Nona needs me . . . and I need to be with her."

"I understand and I think you should move back, too," he said after a long moment. He didn't grill me with questions, but merely gave me a tender look and said he'd talk it over with Mom. "It won't be easy convincing her," he added. "I'm not her favorite person right now."

"You're mine," I said, reaching across to squeeze his hand.

Then he turned on the radio, his favorite oldies station, and hummed along as I closed my eyes and let all my problems roll away.

A sharp musical tone chirped and my eyes snapped open.

"Just my phone," Dad murmured, keeping his gaze ahead on traffic while he reached for his phone.

"Yes? I can't talk now," I heard him say in a sharp tone that startled me. Then he was quiet, listening for a long time. "No. I can't . . . You don't understand . . . Are you sure?"

Energy in the car changed. Dad's aura sparked with fierce energy. Whoever was on the phone was giving him bad news. I knew this instinctively. I even knew that it was a woman, someone close to his age whom he knew well, but was a stranger to me.

"All right! I'll be there!" he snapped. Then he flipped his phone shut and glanced over at me. I kept my eyes closed, sensing that I'd learn more if I pretended to be asleep.

He made a sudden jerk of the wheel and spun around, tires screeching as he changed directions. I tensed, no longer feeling safe and protected.

Where were we going?

I squinted out of the corner of my eyes, noting Dad's serious expression and how he kept glancing over at me anxiously. Something was definitely worrying him—which worried me.

Then we were slowing down, bumping over an uneven road, then curving into a neighborhood where I glimpsed large, overgrown trees closing in over the narrow road. The car stopped.

Dad glanced at me again, then exhaled as if relieved I was asleep.

He stepped out of the car and walked towards a single-story L-shaped yellow house with sagging gutters, a dry lawn of weeds, and faded wood siding.

The door of the house burst open and a woman with long, dry, reddish gray hair and wide hips in a tight leather mini-skirt rushed out to greet him. She had this exhausted look of relief on her face, as if her house was burning and a fireman had just showed up to put out the flames.

She met him on the grass, leaned close, and slipped her arm comfortably around his waist. He didn't push her away, letting her lean on him as if he belonged to her. Her expression was grim, but the way she touched him was too familiar, and something ugly and jealous snarled in me.

Then the door opened again and a girl rushed out of the house so fast that all I could see was long, flaming red hair. I had the sense that she was a few years older than me. She flew down the steps, pushed the woman aside, and flung her arms around my father's neck.

"I knew you'd come!" the girl cried out. "I really need you, Daddy!"

My world slowed and froze to a stop.

Daddy.

She called *my* father "Daddy."

Then she turned in my direction and I saw her face clearly.

My hands flew to my mouth.

Ohmygod.

This couldn't be real. Except for the red hair, she looked just like me.

The End